Janetta Harvey has written two books for adults on living with her dogs rescued from horrible backgrounds. She's a campaigner against puppy farming and the international puppy trade and promotes the adoption of animals.

Annabel Wilson is a primary school teacher and artist. She uses art to promote awareness of the issues involved in puppy farming and pet rescue.

Also by Janetta Harvey

FOR ADULTS

Saving Susie-Belle
Saving One More

Saving Maya

Janetta Harvey

Illustrated by Annabel Wilson

Matador
9 Priory Business Park,
Wistow Road, Kibworth Beauchamp,
Leicestershire. LE8 0RX
Tel: 0116 279 2299
Email: books@troubador.co.uk
Web: www.troubador.co.uk/matador
Twitter: @matadorbooks

ISBN 978 1785893 605

British Library Cataloguing in Publication Data.
A catalogue record for this book is available from the British Library.

Printed and bound by CPI Group (UK) Ltd, Croydon, CR0 4YY
Typeset in 11pt Aldine401 BT by Troubador Publishing Ltd, Leicester, UK

Matador is an imprint of Troubador Publishing Ltd

For Susie-Belle, Juno and Harley.
And dad, who told me to go and get that book written, so I did.

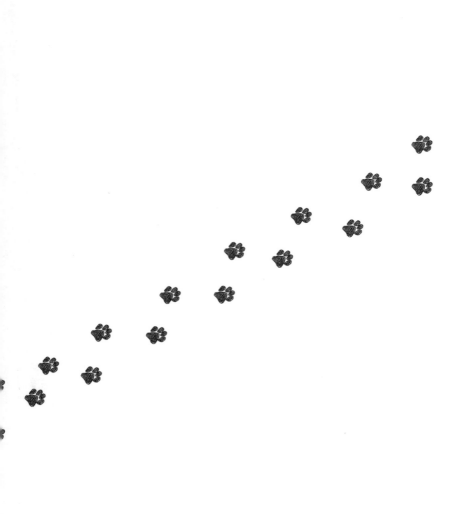

1

Children almost always hang onto
things tighter than their parents think
they will.

E.B. White, *Charlotte's Web*

It was the morning of Willow's first birthday. She woke
up, lifted her nose and knew it was going to be a good
day. Stepping out of bed, she gave herself a long, slow
stretch as she moved across the carpet, and with her
wet, black nose high in the air, took in a deep sniff and
smelled food. Special party food. The air in the bedroom
was rich with the scrumptious smell of freshly cooked
biscuits and goodies from yesterday's baking. It had
wafted all the way up through the house overnight,
deliciously settling into all corners of each room.

As Willow remembered Patsy, busy all yesterday
afternoon, mixing and baking, making all kinds of
tasty things for today's party, her tummy turned over
with happiness, or perhaps it was hunger? Either way,
yesterday had been a happy day: the radio had played
Patsy's favourite songs and more than once she'd done
a little dance and jiggle, smiling over at Willow who'd

1

sat on her soft red cushion, watching from the corner of the sunny kitchen. Willow was happy when Patsy was happy, and both were always happy on baking days. As the afternoon had gone on, Willow knew that if she waited patiently in her bed, Patsy would soon call her over for a taste of the best, her absolute favourite, sardine paste cake topping. She always did.

Willow trusted Patsy not to forget, but just to make sure, as she'd watched Patsy clearing the bowls, she'd given a quiet, soft, woofetty-woof and gentle twitch of her fluffy tail. Patsy stopped what she'd been doing, pushed a long, curly strand of her red hair back from her face and smiling at Willow, had picked up a sticky spoon and called her over. Bouncing across the kitchen floor, tail wagging, skidding to a halt at Patsy's feet, Willow had tipped her grey head back, her bushy white eyebrows twitching with excitement as she'd waited for the bowl. Patsy bent down to Willow's level, she was only a small dog, and held the bowl close to Willow's face. Happily licking the bowl, pink tongue flicking up and down the inside of the bowl, and getting plenty in her thick white beard with her eager slurping, as soon as the bowl was clean she'd looked longingly at the cake which sat cooling on the rack.

"No, you cheeky girl, you'll have to wait for a taste of that," Patsy had smiled, tickling Willow's chin, trying to avoid the sticky blobs in her mucky, now brown-tinged, fishy-smelling beard.

As her mind worked its way back through yesterday's luscious baking marathon, Willow felt peckish and as if to remind her of its emptiness, her tummy grumbled, awaiting its first delight of the day. There was plenty ahead, as Patsy had arranged a birthday celebration with Willow's doggy friends in Kettlecroft Park later, where the cake and other goodies would be shared. Charlie, Alfie, Kai, Ollie, sisters Sookie and Sara, Daisy-Mae and Darcie were all going to be there. These were Willow's best friends, not counting Patsy, who was her very best friend, but as she wasn't a dog she fell into a different friend category.

Of all her friends, Charlie was the eldest of the Kettlecroft Park gang, an old, slow dog who liked nothing better than snoozing on his bed once the park had been visited each morning. Apart from Charlie, and Sara who was also getting on a bit in age, most of Willow's friends loved chasing, which was her favourite game. Ollie was the fastest and no-one could catch him but they all liked to try. He was also obsessed with crows. Willow heard it said by the humans who knew him, that it was the terrier in Ollie that fuelled his crow-obsession.

Then there was Alfie, a bigger, lumbering dog usually found with his pal, Kai, busy rough and tumbling together. Sara's younger sister Sookie, was almost as fast as Ollie. She was a short-legged but quick-running black and white terrier cross, a bit smaller than Willow, who loved nothing better than a wild game of chase.

Each morning, if Willow had arrived first, when she spotted Sookie across the park coming in, she lay flat on her belly, keeping her head low with eyes fixed as Sookie lifted her nose, catching the smells wafting on the fresh morning air. Then, the second she caught Willow's sweet odour, her eyes began searching, her tail wag getting faster as she started moving towards the spot where she thought

4

Willow was. As soon as she was spotted by Sookie, Willow stood up, tail wagging hard and they both rushed across the grass. Racing headlong towards one another, just when they looked like they might collide…

… WHOOOSH!

Sookie took a swerve to the left and Willow to the right, and they ran in a circle back to face each other, tails wagging hard and happy… and off they would chase again, hurtling around the park. Every morning was the same. They loved their simple, energetic game.

All this awaited Willow later on, and she was eager to get to Kettlecroft Park to share her cake and Patsy's baking with her friends, as well as a romp and chase. But, first she needed to wake up Patsy so her birthday could start. Standing on her back legs, her front paws gripping the crisp, white duvet she peered over the edge of the big bed. Just within her reach, if she stretched a little white paw forward, was Patsy's sleeping face, hidden underneath the blanket of her curly red hair. Willow shifted her feet to bring herself closer to the bed, stretched her left paw as far forward as she could, and smacked Patsy's nose.

"Ouch!" Patsy was startled awake. "Morning cheeky," she yawned, rubbing her nose and moving back from the edge of the bed. "I guess it's time to wake up?" she said, on the end of a big yawn, running one hand through her messy mop of hair.

"Come on then, up you come," she patted the bed inviting Willow up for their morning cuddle.

This was one of Willow's favourite things in the world, squeezing into Patsy's arms for long, cosy snuggles. It reminded Willow of being with her mum, before she came to live with Patsy. With her mum, when she wasn't playing with her brothers and sisters, they'd all nestle together in their bed, pushing in close and snuggly. She had three grey and white sisters and two black brothers, and for the first eight weeks after they were born, they'd all lived with a kind human family, of mum, dad and two sisters.

Willow remembered Abbey and Emily each morning, the sisters taking turns to pick her up, stroking her and whispering into her floppy grey ears how much they loved her. It had made her feel all soft and squishy inside. But on some days, Emily would add, "We love you but we can't keep you forever." This had always worried Willow: if they weren't keeping her, where was she going?

But she needn't have worried, for the day came when Patsy turned up at the house for the first time. With Abbey and Emily holding in their small, caring hands Willow's sisters, softly stroking the tops of the puppies' heads and down along their backs, their mum handed Willow to Patsy. Willow remembered the first thing she noticed was Patsy's new, interesting smell, and Willow wanted to check it out more, to fill her tiny black nose with the strange aroma. She'd nuzzled into the green softness of Patsy's scarf to reach the bare skin of her neck to get a deeper sniff. It was such a delicious smell, it reached deep down into Willow's body and a feeling of warm sweetness filled her. She was so happy, she wriggled herself away from Patsy's neck to give her face a big, drippy, wet lick with her pink tongue.

"Oh, you little darling," Patsy had giggled as she'd given Willow's chin a gentle rub and tickle.

After a few more minutes cuddling Willow, Patsy put her carefully back with her mum and brothers. Willow playfully tugged on her brother's ears while their mum kept careful watch over her babies playing. Patsy then gave each of Willow's sisters a cuddle before sitting down with Willow's human mum to talk. They had talked and talked, it seemed to go on forever, questions flying between the two women, back and forth, so many questions, a lot of details needed talking about. It seemed to Willow that whatever was happening was important to everyone. One question was followed by another. After all the questions

had been asked and answered on both sides, Patsy had one last cuddle of Willow, who loved all the attention, before leaving and saying she'd be back to see her.

After Patsy's first visit, she came again to see Willow, and then, on the third time, she brought with her a small soft, comfy crate. Abbey had put Willow's pink blanket in the crate and Emily slotted in one of the soft toys that Willow liked playing with. This had puzzled Willow, but she was pleased to see Patsy again, who had smiled and chatted a lot to the girls, who were not their usual bubbly selves, but quiet and subdued.

Then, as if she needed to do it before she had time to think more about her actions, Abbey had suddenly picked Willow up, given her a big cuddle, and squashing her face into Willow's neck had said, "Now you be a good girl Willow, Patsy's going to love you very much. She's promised us she's going to take great care of you."

Emily took Willow in her arms, a big fat tear running down one cheek, "Willow we love you loads, but Patsy's going to be your family now, and she's going to make sure you have everything you need," Emily sniffed onto the top of Willow's head as she handed her to Patsy.

Taking Willow into her arms, Patsy had given everyone a rueful smile, popped Willow into her soft crate and off they headed to start their new life together.

All that had been almost a year ago, and yet it seemed like yesterday to Willow.

"We've had a great first year together haven't we?" Patsy seemed to read her mind as her long fingers stroked Willow's ears. "Here's to many more," she said as she brushed her lips across the top of her furry friend's head.

2

If more of us valued food and cheer and
song above hoarded gold, it would be a
merrier world.

J.R.R. Tolkien, *The Hobbit*

"Morning birthday girl," Patsy's friend Tom called, as
he came through the back door into the sunny kitchen.
"Go on then, take your pick," he grinned, his blue eyes
twinkling as he put a large box full of presents on the
floor in front of Willow, who was excited to see him any
day of the week, but on her birthday was super ditsy.
She bounced about under his feet, dashing between
the box and him as he bent down and gave her face and
ears a vigorous rub, making her snuffle and snort with
excitement. She loved Tom, he was always fun, and keen
to play a game with her.

As Tom straightened himself up, Willow's interest
turned to the box: it smelled good enough to eat, and she
tore into it, shredding it away from the treasure trove of
presents it contained. This was a lot of fun. One by one,
Willow picked out a package, getting more excited as she
worked her way through them all. She tore off layers of

red and white polka dot wrapping paper, revealing soft toys, including an octopus, a squirrel, a squeaky ball and a big squashy rubber duck and there, at the bottom, a huge delicious smelling bag of tasty, chewy treats.

"Oh no you don't, you can have those later," Patsy smiled, swiftly taking the bag from Willow's mouth, placing it high up on a shelf beside a pile of plates, out of Willow's reach. Willow was mighty confused. Why couldn't she eat the lot right now? It was her birthday, it was her present, and she was a pretty peckish. But, no point pondering the oddities of humans, not when there was a pile of new things to enjoy and she turned back to her heap of gifts. The fun was only just starting as she dug into the mound of toys that had been covered in thick sheets of crinkly, crackly paper. In fact, shredding the paper and racing around the kitchen with scraps in her mouth was almost as much fun as reaching the toys hidden inside.

"I think she likes that one," Tom laughed, as Willow grabbed the fluffy, soft squirrel, chomping on it to make it squeal and squeak. She flipped it over her head, getting more and more excited as she spun around, grabbing it up again in her mouth before flipping it over her back once more, and this time it landed in the centre of the huge pile of torn wrapping paper. The excitement continued as she couldn't decide whether to play with the squirrel, or the paper, and she dug her furry face deeper into the slippery paper trying to get hold of the disappearing squirrel. It was all a lot of fun.

As she bounced between Patsy and Tom sitting at the table, and back to her bed with the squirrel clamped firmly in her mouth, she realised it gave out a louder squeak if she got the squeeze in her teeth just in the right position. Just to be certain that it was more fun than the paper, Willow grabbed a mouthful of shredded paper and jumped up onto the window seat and back down onto the kitchen mat, trailing red and white paper shreds behind her before settling on her bed with the squirrel.

"You funny little thing," Patsy laughed, handing Tom a cup of tea and slice of buttered toast.

"Reckon I could've just wrapped up a ball of newspaper and she'd have been perfectly happy," Tom smiled at Willow who right then, was burying the squirrel under the piles of torn wrapping paper she had dragged into her bed.

"She's a happy dog, she really is," Patsy replied.

"Any more thoughts on getting her a sister?" Tom asked and Willow's ears pricked up, her head tilted first to the left, then over to the right so she could better hear this interesting chat. A sister? For her? This sounded good. Her friends Sara and Sookie were sisters and they had so much fun together. Imagine waking up and having a friend to hang out with straight away each day, no need to wait to meet up in Kettlecroft Park. Yes, a sister sounded a jolly good idea.

"Well I've been looking," Patsy said, her smile fading. "I've decided not to buy another puppy, there are just so many dogs who need homes, who people don't want any more and it breaks my heart."

Willow's eyes opened wider as her head tilted back the other way, she never liked to see Patsy not happy and right then, Patsy seemed a little sad.

"It's really horrible how many dogs get given away every year, I honestly can't think of buying another puppy when I know there must be a perfect dog just waiting for me to find her and bring her here to live with us," Patsy said, looking down at Willow who sat listening hard.

"Really? You sure about this?" Tom frowned. "Wouldn't a puppy be a lot easier than getting a rescue dog you know nothing about?" he asked.

"Well, not really, a puppy takes a lot of work, and a dog that's been rehomed can be perfectly easy to live with. They often just need a second chance, there's not always a problem with them," Patsy replied, pushing her long curly hair back from her face. "Yep, my mind's made up. I've spent hours looking into it and there's no need at all for me to buy a puppy. There are loads of good dogs in rescue centres… puppies even, if I want one, but I don't think I do."

Patsy patted her knees and Willow crossed the tiled floor to sit in front of her, tail wagging, happier as Patsy seemed happy once again. She tipped her chin forward just a little so it rested on Patsy's lap, her dark brown, almost black eyes looking up adoringly at Patsy who smiled and gave the furry grey top of her head a soft kiss. This all sounded excellent to Willow. If she understood Patsy and Tom right, and she was pretty sure she did, a new friend, a sister was going to come and live with her and Patsy. This was the best birthday surprise yet.

"But puppies are a lot of fun," Tom said, putting his mug of tea down on the kitchen table so he could give Willow a stroke, as she shifted her head from resting on Patsy's knees to nuzzle in between them both.

Patsy sighed. "Puppies are cute, I agree. But they don't stay puppies for long anyway, and really, I've come across some horrible stuff on the internet about how a lot of puppies start their lives. They're not all lucky like Willow you know, born with kind families, in a nice home," Patsy stood up and looked out of the window, her hazel eyes focusing on the large clump of white snowdrops under the trees at the end of the garden. Turning back to Tom, she said, "Have you heard about puppy farming?"

"Puppy farming? Errr, nope, but whatever it is, it doesn't sound good."

"It's horrible," Patsy said. "Dogs are kept in sheds, or barns for years, their lives are miserable. They're kept so they can produce puppies, that's all. They're not taken care of, they're never cuddled, their food's basic and sometimes they never see a person for days."

"Really? That's terrible."

"It really is, I've been digging about to find out more and it's shocking. The dogs don't go for walks… gosh the poor things never see daylight. They're basically kept as prisoners their whole lives," Patsy sipped her tea and offered Tom more from the pot.

Tom shook his head. "Sounds awful. I've kind of heard of it but… "

"It's so sad it makes me want to cry when I see what happens behind the sweet puppies we see for sale everywhere," Patsy's eyes moistened as she put her empty mug in the sink.

"I never knew it was so awful" Tom said, standing to give her a hug.

Pulling away, Patsy sniffed, blew her nose into a tissue, took a deep breath and was fired up to tell him more, "It's hard to believe it happens but it does. And all so that puppies can be sold in pet shops or by other people, puppy dealers basically. Sometimes the puppies get taken from their mums in the puppy farms and are sold in homes by people pretending they've been born in the house," she sighed, sitting down at the table.

"It's just awful. Poor mum gets left behind in a dirty shed, without her puppies, or anyone to take care of her," Patsy wrapped her arms around herself and squeezed, as if trying to comfort herself as she looked down at Willow, a look of sadness on her face.

"I'm so pleased I did my homework when I brought you home Willow," she said. "It's a horrible business," she said, looking at Tom, "one way I'll know for sure I'm not being part of it, will be to rehome a dog who's in a rescue centre, one who really needs a home. I'm not buying a puppy, I'm not risking supporting a puppy farm, or falling into the hands of a dealer."

"Well you're selling the idea pretty well to me." Tom leaned forwards, put his arms around her and hugged her tight.

"When you think about it, the puppies are the lucky ones," she sighed into his shoulder, "at least they get out and go to live in families."

"Bit different from Willow's life eh?" Tom said as he sat back, reaching out to stroke Willow who sat watching them, wondering at the conversation she was struggling to understand.

"Oh Tom, really it's awful, the poor mums and dads

are trapped forever. They don't get to leave. They're the ones who really suffer. Some of what I've been finding out makes me really cross. And sad. How can anyone do it to dogs?"

Patsy was overcome by the love she suddenly felt for Willow and scooping her up into her arms, Patsy gave her a tight squeeze.

"Imagine if you were there Willow, stuck in a puppy farm. I can't bear to think of it. But now I know about it, we're going to do something good. We're going to give a home to a dog in need. I think we're going to bring one of the mums to live with us," Patsy breathed into Willow's sweet smelling fur.

3

I want very much to believe that there's
a heaven, that death is not a full stop, and
that we will all see one another again.
Michael Morpurgo, *Private Peaceful*

The pain in my hips today is worse than ever. I move
around trying to get comfortable on the cold, hard
concrete floor of the barn where I've spent my whole
life. I don't know how old I am, but I've been here a long
time. I was born in this dark barn and I will probably die
here. I've never been outside. The furthest I've moved
was when I was taken from my mum when I was a few
months old. She lived a few pens along from where I am,
here in the barn. She must be dead now, although I can't
be certain. I haven't seen her since the day the Man took
me from her.

It was the first time that I'd left the concrete pen I
shared with my mum and I was frightened. All around
me I could hear barking, crying dogs. The barn is an
unhappy place. As the Man marched me through the
huge shed past all the pens I was terrified. I never saw
my mum again as the Man took me to another pen, with

a thin scattering of grubby sawdust on the floor and a lot of other dogs who I didn't know. We were all scared and huddled together for comfort.

In the first few weeks after leaving my mum, in the middle of the lonely nights, I cried and cried into the dark for her. Sometimes, just sometimes, I thought I could hear a faint answer coming back. I could never be certain that it was my mum, there are always so many sounds in the barn it can be hard to hear one thing from another, but it gave me some comfort thinking she might be answering my cries. Then, as time went by, I stopped crying for her, and her voice stopped. Whether it had been in my head, or somewhere in the barn, I'm never sure. But I am sure now that she's no longer nearby. Something that's hard for me to explain, it's an emptiness, a hollowness in my heart that tells me she's gone. Even if I try really hard to remember, I can't recall what she sounded, or looked like. There's just deathly silence in my head where she used to be.

Although the barn is never silent. It's a noisy place. The air is filled with the sounds of dogs barking, crying, yelping, whining and howling. Older dogs whimper from pain, the younger ones bark from boredom and loneliness. And then there's the puppies. The hungry, scared puppies are painful to hear day after day, night after night. The sounds of sorrow and suffering crash around the walls of the barn all day, all night.

I try to get a little more comfortable but it's hard when there's nothing but concrete to rest on. I'm hoping that soon, spring will arrive and bring with it the warmer weather. This winter has been long and hard. Many

mornings I've woken from a bad night of storms and heavy rain battering the tin roof of the barn. On some stormy nights, the wind blasted the barn walls, causing noise like I've never experienced. I've been terrified, cowering in the corner of my pen, hearing the sounds of the storm outside, matched by the wailing and terror-filled sounds of the dogs all around me, although I cannot see them. Many a night I've wanted to die. To be released from this life I'm forced to live. And then, morning arrives and I find I'm still here, alive but wishing I was dead.

When my back and hips ache like they do today, I long for the warmer days as my aching bones feel better when the weather is warmer. But then it gets too warm, and the barn soon overheats and the air gets hotter, and smellier and dustier. I get so thirsty and crave a cool, fresh bowl of water, instead of the dirty, green sludge that's in my pen. With the rising heat, the flies come visiting in their thousands, buzzing about, driving the dogs mad. And the insects creep and crawl through our food.

But right now, as the cold creeps into my body and I can't stop shivering with cold and hunger, some warmth would be nice. These days, the Man seems to forget that I'm here as he walks past my pen without glancing in. It's not that I want him to see me, oh no, not that, he's nasty and mean, but I do want some food. I'm hungry and it must be a few days since I last ate. I lose track of time, it drags so, and days run into nights and nights into days without there being anything to mark one from the other. The dark of the barn makes sure of that.

There was never much food to eat, but now there are some days I have nothing at all. The water in the dirty bowl is almost gone. I don't remember when it was last filled with fresh water. I take the smallest sips of the mucky sludge, as I made the mistake once of taking great gulps of the fresh water when it arrived, but then no more was brought for days. I licked the last drops from the dirty bowl, desperately seeking more. I felt like I was dying of thirst as it was hot and stuffy in the barn. It must have been summer. From then on, I learnt to be careful never to drink the last drop, but to save some in case I'm forgotten about again. Which looks like it's happening now. Over time, I've got used to feeling thirsty. As I take a tiny sip of sludge, I make myself imagine that I'm really taking a big fat drink of clean, running water. It eases the pain of my dry mouth and throat just for a second, before the reality comes back and my parched tongue reminds me I'm just dreaming.

4

It is only with the heart that one can see rightly. What is essential is invisible to the eye.

Antoine de Saint-Exupéry, *The Little Prince*

"Are you ready? Shall we go?" Patsy called, as Willow lay busily sorting through her new toys. At that exact moment, she was chomping away on each of the eight soft felt legs of her new orange and blue octopus, trying to work out which one squeaked the loudest. Undecided, and distracted by Patsy's call to go, she dropped it behind the wicker toy basket where she'd left the squirrel a little earlier, saving them both for further inspection when she returned from her party in Kettlecroft Park.

Padding quickly across the room into the hallway where Tom was gathering the door keys, Willow ran over and sat at Patsy's feet, waiting for her to clip on her brand new red leather lead. This was another birthday gift from Tom. It held no interest for Willow, despite Patsy excitedly squealing with joy when she'd carefully unwrapped it. In fact, Willow had been a little disappointed it hadn't been something tasty to eat, as the package had smelt temptingly good. Although, she did admit, it was a rather smart lead. Ahh well, she was happy, that Patsy was happy, with Tom's peculiar idea of what made a good doggy present. And she'd instantly forgiven his curious choice of fancy-red-dog-lead-as-gift when, with her teeth and claws working quickly together, she'd ripped the wrapping paper on the next present and out from the shreds of red tissue, fell the octopus. Now, that was what Willow called a present as it plopped onto the mat.

"Come on then, let's go see your friends," said Patsy, leading Willow out of the door and down the garden path to the wooden front gate. In her left hand, she was carrying a large basket, stuffed with a selection of home baked dog biscuits in plastic tubs. There was a good number of peanut butter, banana and oat cookies; these were Willow's favourites, and a generous sized tin of delicious squares of liver cake, made from Patsy's special recipe her friend Kate had given her. All Willow's doggy friends loved liver cake. Patsy had only to open the smallest corner of the bag containing the neat little brown cubes of tasty delight, and over would run every dog within smelling distance; even Barney the bulldog who rarely ran anywhere.

But the best thing of all was in the box being carried by Tom. As Willow trotted along between them, she fought the urge to leap at Tom's legs and reach up with her nose and take deep, long sniffs of the pink boxed parcel he was holding carefully in his arms. All morning in the house its aromas had enticed her black wet nose, making it twitch and itch with excitement every time her

nostrils captured a whiff. But the neat box had been kept well out of Willow's reach, high up on a kitchen shelf.

But now it was close by, and Willow knew that inside the pretty pink, cardboard cocoon sat the star of yesterday's baking. The smells coming out of the box were so yummy Willow was finding it hard to control herself. What she really wanted to do, but which she knew she mustn't, was to jump up and grab it from Tom's arms, rip into the parcel and expose the treasure hiding inside: her birthday cake. Her delicious, mouth-wateringly good – if you're a dog – sardine and carrot cake with its moist, tongue-tingling fishy paste topping.

While she struggled to focus less on the cake, and more on walking nicely on the lead neatly beside Tom's legs, Willow thought about how much her pals at the park were going to love the squishy, whiffy concoction of a cake. But if they didn't, she was sure she'd be able to eat the whole thing herself. No doubt about it. She could eat cake all day if only Patsy allowed it. Come to think of it, why didn't she? Such silly rules humans made her live by.

Kettlecroft Park was a short walk from Willow's house, along a quiet footpath where every morning and evening Willow checked the messages left by all the neighbourhood dogs. Sniff, sniff, pee, pee. Even though this was Willow's birthday, and she had a few other things on her mind, like cake, her new presents left at home, and all the biscuits she was going to eat, the path still needed checking.

"There you go," Patsy unclipped her lead and she was off, nose to the ground, heading straight to the closest grassy tussock. As she buried her face deep into the lush greenness, she inhaled a huge nose-full of wonderful whiffs. She was giddy with excitement and all thoughts of cake flew from her mind as the heady smells rising from the grass took over. Willow's first moments on the footpath were always the same: one hundred percent nose focus, it was as if her other senses had switched off, as she heard nothing, saw nothing, said nothing, but smelt everything. She sought out every tiny drop of aroma and decoded the hidden messages left by all the different creatures who'd passed along the path since her last visit.

Of most interest were the dogs' smells. Willow found these easiest to understand. Here was Charlie's pee, he must have been along already to leave his message. Now,

who had he marked over? Whose was that interesting, musky scent? Willow took another deeper sniff, trying to ignore Charlie's smell, and get below it, to the curious tones lying underneath his big scented pee. It could be… no surely not… Sneakers the Cat! Odd, he's not usually found on this corner, Willow thought. This is a dangerous spot for him to stop, being the place where all dogs gather and linger on their way to the park.

What Willow couldn't know, and her nose was detecting but her brain wasn't decoding, was that last night while the neighbourhood dogs were all tucked up in their warm beds, Sneakers the Cat sat for five long minutes on this corner. He enjoyed the peace of the spot that the dogs claimed for themselves during the daytime. With his black furry bottom sat comfortably on the thick grass cushion, he had slowly closed his green eyes, tipped back his sleek black head, revealing the white heart-shaped spot on his velvet throat, and taken a long, slow sniff of the cool night air. Unlike the hurried, excitable smelling the dogs did, Sneakers sat almost motionless, drawing in through his snub pink nose, chilled air which carried all the day's fragrance deep into his mind. He took his time, allowing his brain to filter through the many messages that were bouncing around on the air his nose expertly pulled in.

Dogs, lots of smelly dogs. That's what the messages told Sneakers the Cat, as he opened his sharp, bright, emerald eyes and looked up at the starry sky. Dogs bumbling along the path, on their way to the park to run around in pointless frenzies, sometimes chasing balls and other times just each other and, that silly white one always chasing the crows. Didn't he know birds are not for playing with but for killing? Perched high on the fence that bordered the path and overlooked the park, Sneakers liked to watch the dogs. They never knew he was up there, above them. Although, as they passed by on the path below, just before reaching the main Kettlecroft Park Gate, some did. Some noticed his presence. It was always the sharper ones who caught his scent and stopped, heads tipping back, lifting their twitching noses, looking around, searching for the source of the feline fragrance, before being hurried along by their humans. Last night, when he'd finished taking in the scented messages from the cold night air, Sneakers had smugly sat awhile longer, enjoying the fact he was a cat and needed no human to walk the path with him, hurrying him along, like the silly daft dogs did.

Willow was baffled by Sneakers' lingering smell from

last night at that grassy spot on the corner of the path. She couldn't work it out. It was cat, definitely cat, but no cat sat there long enough to leave behind so much scent. Oh well, with a shake of her grey head, she moved on, continuing along the path, carefully checking, smell by smell who else had been along, trying to forget the mystery whiff of a cat, sat where no cat usually did.

5

> He now felt glad at having suffered
> sorrow and trouble, because it enabled
> him to enjoy so much better all the
> pleasure and happiness around him
> > Hans Christian Andersen,
> > *The Ugly Duckling*

As Willow made her way along the footpath, the overwhelming excitement of all the smells started to settle. Moving farther away from the stinging concentration of those left on the corner, it made room in her nose for the softer, more familiar messages which wafted up from the grassy edges of the path. As her mind calmed, she found herself thinking back to what she'd heard Patsy and Tom talking about in the house. Patsy had spoken about sad dogs living as prisoners in puppy farms just to make puppies. Did that mean that they never got to do as she was doing right then? Enjoying the smells of the open air, the scents left along a grassy footpath by all the local dogs, foxes, mice, rats and the odd cat passing through?

Could there really be dogs, thousands if what Patsy

said was right, trapped in barns and sheds, who never got to see, or smell anything outside? Willow shuddered as she trotted along, trying to shake the feeling of sadness she felt for all those poor, lonely dogs.

But the feeling wouldn't go away, and the questions kept pushing into her mind. What did the dogs do all day? Where did they go to the toilet? What did they eat? Willow wondered if they had any toys. She didn't think they did if what Patsy told Tom was true. How could a dog be happy with no toys? And if they had no toys, did this mean they never played games? The dogs were prisoners in tiny dark spaces, with concrete floors and walls. No soft beds. No beds at all. Just the floor with some dirty sawdust Patsy had said. No cuddles... no love... no-one who cared for them.

Then there were the other places, and this made Willow feel very sad indeed, she'd heard Patsy whisper to Tom, places where dogs lived for years in wire cages. Cages? Surely Patsy had that wrong. How can dogs live in cages?

Willow's mind was buzzing as she walked along, thinking about the mums of the puppies never getting to leave the barns. So sad that they were left all alone after their puppies were taken away. She thought back to when she left her mum and came to live with Patsy. She remembered taking one last look back and seeing her mum being cuddled tightly by Emily, with Abbey crouching on her other side, gently stroking her mum's ears, dropping kisses on her beautiful, furry head. She hated to think that her mum would have been left all alone, with no-one to love her when her puppies had gone off to their new homes. How awful for all the mums in the puppy farms if that was the case. How terribly alone and sad they must feel.

As Willow's thoughts jumped about in her busy brain, her heart was heavy with sadness for all the dogs who suffered in the world. She could hear Patsy and Tom chattering a few foot steps behind her, and she felt glad that she was loved by them; loved, safe and free to enjoy her life.

All thoughts of puppy farms and sad dogs flew from her young mind, as she arrived at the park and ran full speed through the wrought iron gates, leaving Patsy and Tom to follow behind. Willow never hesitated to enter the park, she felt as at home there as she did in her own garden; it was where she could hang out with her friends and today was extra exciting as most would be there for her party. Straight away, across the grass, she spotted her friend Sookie waiting for her. Racing across the damp, slightly muddy ground to greet her, she was delighted to also find that their old friend Charlie had come out to join them.

Charlie was ancient, nobody knew exactly how old, but he was at least fifteen. These days, he was slow and slept a lot, but when he was younger, Charlie had been a frisky dog, full of mischief and high energy. Each day, nothing had tired him out. From first thing in the morning, to last thing at night, he'd be looking for something to do; he'd been a busy, boisterous dog in his time. This, however, had brought Charlie trouble and sorrow. Bought as a puppy by his first family, they'd showered him with love for the first few months; he'd enjoyed lots of games and walks and his memories of those days were good. Many a time in the park, Willow had listened to tales of his happy early days with his first family.

Then, after a year or so, Charlie's walks had got less and less and the games had dwindled to nothing. Days went by when he'd be left at home for hours all alone, with little to do and no-one for company. Some days he felt he'd explode with boredom, and he once told Willow of a day when instead of exploding, he'd chewed up the skirting board in the lounge. This had got him into a lot of trouble, and tempers had erupted when his family returned and saw what he'd done. Not long after this incident, a lady had come to the house and taken him away with her. She was kind, and as she hugged Charlie tight their first night together, she'd told him that he'd be staying with her until his new family was found. This had mighty confused Charlie; why did he need a new family? What was wrong with his old one?

As the lady stroked and hugged him, he listened hard to what she told him, trying to understand what was happening. He knew he'd been bad for chewing the skirting board, but if he'd been for a walk that day he was certain he wouldn't have done it. All he wanted was a walk and some company. He was a little sad as he never got to say goodbye to his family, but, the lady was nice and she took good care of him. Their days together were spent walking on the hills, and she taught him some fun tricks. Each day he was happy and tired, and never felt the urge to chew stuff left around the house. Especially not her skirting boards.

Then, one morning he woke up to find a new family was coming to take him to live by the sea. This family was a lot of fun for Charlie, he had long walks on the beach, and he tried rock pooling with them for the first time in his life. They seemed to like his boundless energy and encouraged his wild side. They were happy days. Until, one day, a baby arrived in the house. And once again, the family didn't spend as much time with Charlie. The trips to the beach became rarer and shorter, no more dawdling in rock pools for Charlie. Once more, his days inside the house were long and boring. It felt ominously familiar to him. Only, this time, a lady didn't take him away to her house, his family took him to a kennel.

When he'd sat in the park one chilly day last autumn and told Willow his life story, with deep sighs and sadness, he said he remembered well, the day he left the beach family. It was in the summer, the days were long and hot and the family took the baby off on their holiday abroad – without Charlie. He was in the kennel, waiting for their return and he wasn't too worried, a little sad at being left behind, but he'd been there before and they always came back for him. Only, that summer, they didn't. As the weeks passed, and the summer came to an end, he waited every day for his family to return. He woke every morning hoping it would be the day they came, but they never did. The staff in the kennels were kind to Charlie, but he longed for his old family to come and take him home and out to the beach again.

Many people came and looked at him while he stayed in the kennels, but no-one wanted him. He heard people saying he was a bit ugly, and old, which made him sad as he didn't feel old, he just felt bored and lonely. He'd stayed for over a year in the kennels, and then, eight years ago Stuart and Di who lived in Kettlecroft Avenue had visited the kennel. Di had immediately fallen in love with Charlie's sad face and taken him home with them.

Charlie told Willow that he'd done his best to be a good boy for Di and Stuart, he really didn't want to go back to the kennel. Each morning he woke up, he hoped he was going to be allowed to stay. Di and Stuart certainly made lots of promises to him, they never seemed to tire of telling Charlie how much they loved him. After a long while, maybe a year or so, he let himself believe that they really meant it, and that he'd be staying with them for good. It all seemed a long time ago, a different lifetime in fact, and yet, these days they still promised him every day when they went to bed that he was their special boy and they loved him more than they could say. And he was there to stay, forever.

These days, all that was a distant memory as it was all he could do to potter over to the park, flop down on the grass and watch the youngsters enjoying themselves. It made him tingle with warmth to see them all running and having fun. It helped him to remember his days running on the beach and rock pooling. When Willow was a young puppy and had first met Charlie she'd been a little too lively for his liking and in his gentlemanly way he'd taught her to be a bit calmer around him and the other older dogs she met. His important lessons had helped her settle into the Kettlecroft Park gang. She loved being with the younger dogs and their chasing and running, but she often joined the older, quieter dogs to listen to their tales. Willow, always keen to learn, got along well with Charlie, she respected him and once she'd learnt not to rush up to him, but to save that high energy for her pal Sookie, she loved to sit and absorb Charlie's wise words.

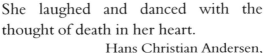

6

She laughed and danced with the thought of death in her heart.

Hans Christian Andersen,
The Little Mermaid

Last night I slept badly. I never sleep well, there's too much noise in the barn with dogs barking and crying, whining and whimpering, yipping and yapping. It's hard to get comfortable on the concrete, but last night was worse than usual. My tummy ached with hunger and I couldn't get my mind to rest. Memories kept creeping in, each time I was about to drop off to sleep, an image from the past came to me and jolted me awake.

My night time memories aren't all bad, although most are. Last night my puppies came tip-toeing into my mind, bringing with them a moment of sweetness that I'd forgotten existed. As I let my exhausted self, drift into the memory, I saw once again, with my mind's eye, their fresh, innocent faces. Tiny black features all squished up with eyes closed to the world.

Their days with me were spent feeding and sleeping, till their bright little eyes were ready to open and explore their small, new world. Eyes that blinked and struggled to open and close as the chinks of light coming through holes in the barn roof hit their startled unfamiliar gaze.

Their world was dull, with nothing to fill the days. But their wish to play was strong and together each litter would make the best of what they had, which was me and one another. There has never been anything else in this concrete pen for my puppies to play with. No toys. Nothing. It's a barren start to life for puppies born here.

Last night, in the fleeting kind memories my mind allowed, I conjured visions of my pups playfully chewing one another's ears, tumbling about together on the hard grubby floor, having fun in the only way they knew how. Those had been happy moments, set amid a mass of horribleness. And the dark cloak of bleak reality came, blotting out any traces of joy in my puppies' lives as I remembered the filth of the floor, their tiny paws stepping into the smelly muck, poop and pee. It disgusts me to have to live, sleep, eat and toilet in the same small space but what choice do I have? Or my pups?

Every once in a while, suddenly, noisily the Man comes, banging into each pen in the barn, with the dreaded noise of spraying water. I hate those days, and I'm glad they are rare. When he gets to my cell, he doesn't bother seeing where I am first, instead, he squirts in the powerful jet of cold water. If I get in the way, it's just too bad. When I was young, I used to rush around the pen trying to dodge the hateful blast of cold water. I'd scuttle into the corners, flying from one concrete wall to the other, hating it when the force of the water caught me. Which it always did.

Then, as quickly as he arrives the Man goes, leaving the floor wet, still stinking of years of filth and muck. I don't know why he bothers. I'm always left soggy and cold as there's no escaping the spraying hose, however hard I might try. These days, although I'm terrified of being caught in the lethal force of the spray, I'm too weak to move fast, so stay where I am. I put up with the chilly drenching, and hope it will soon be over.

I look at myself and know that my coat is thick with the reek of my own waste and I hate myself for it. I know this is wrong, I know a dog should not live this way. When I was younger I tried cleaning myself as best I could. I'd pull with my teeth at the knots in my dull, grey fur which was caked in grime and poop. But now I'm so tired and weak, it's hard to do it, and my teeth are sore and rotten and the effort is too much. I look down at my legs and see straggly long hair, clogged with knots and stained yellow with my pee. My feet are painful as my black nails have grown so long they are curling in and digging into my skin, I'm ashamed of the state I'm in. I wish my life was better. Or over.

Maybe it's because I feel that my end might be close that my mind is filled with memories of my babies. All the many puppies I've given birth to in the long years I've spent in this place. I've loved them all for the short time they've been allowed to stay with me. I've fed and cared for each of them and cherished every single one. But I never got to see any of them happy for long, or to love them for more than a short while, as they've been taken from me, litter by litter and I've been left all alone once again. On my own with a heart filled with grief.

The first time the Man came and took away my puppies, I thought they'd be coming back to me. How could I know that I would never see them again and be left alone in the cell? Or that this would happen again and again to me through many years? And each time it happened my lonely heart would break a little more.

7

Life is more fun if you play games.
Roald Dahl, *My Uncle Oswald*

In Kettlecroft Park Willow's birthday party was well underway. All her friends had turned out to enjoy themselves. Kai, a big, brown and white shaggy dog, and Alfie schnauzer, were racing around, running, chasing, lunging towards and away from each other with lightning speed. The rain of a few days earlier had made the grass soft. As they flung themselves around, they churned it up into a muddy mess, in turn, making themselves grubbier, and happier by the minute. They loved every muddy moment of their frolicking. Willow loved these games, but was less keen on being mucky than the others. But she still ran to and fro amid the big dogs' boisterous activity, just managing to stay out from under their feet, as she barked noisy encouragement from the side-lines. When she'd had enough of that, she dashed, panting, over to her quieter friends who were pottering by the picnic table Tom had set out.

"Darcie, what you got there?" Willow asked her brindle coloured friend who was chewing something quite manky looking. Something dead and ripe, with a long, thin tail, Willow thought, as she got a little closer.

"Oh, sshhmmunfink I ppffound," mumbled Darcie, grinding hard on whatever it was she'd found on the ground, over by the iron-gate as she'd come in. With the 'something' half in, half out of her mouth, she turned her head away from Willow, gave one last big crunch with her strong staffie jaws and swallowed whatever it had been.

"That was good. Found it as I came in, think it might have been a rat, not sure, hard to tell the state it was in. Haven't had one of them for a bit," said Darcie, turning back with a grin.

"A rat?" Willow asked, bewildered by her friend's culinary tastes. Darcie was always on the scrounge for something to eat, but foraging for rats felt a bit too odd. Willow knew that cats ate mice and rats, but did dogs?

39

Darcie was renowned as the 'Kettlecroft Guzzler' and gobbled up anything she found. And she never seemed to be any the worse for wear; she'd never had a day of illness in her life.

"Tough as old boots, soft as a pudding," Colin, her human friend always said when people were alarmed at her gobbling up all kinds of rubbish around the park.

Willow hoped that Tom had put her cake somewhere safely out of Darcie's reach. She feared she'd be left with none for herself once Darcie got a taste of its fishy deliciousness.

"Hang on, hang on," Darcie suddenly said, moving her shoulders wide, her back legs a little wider. A weird look passed over her face, and just as Willow started to feel worried at her friend's unusual stance and staring look,

BBBRRRRUUURRRRRRP!

… up came a belch from the depths of Darcie's strong, stocky body. The stench knocked Willow back a step.

"Wow! You ok?" she asked, as Darcie took a gulp of air.

"That's better," Darcie smiled, pleased to have cleared the noxious gas from her gut. "Hhhm. Rat. Yep, definitely rat, now I remember, same thing happened before. Terrible for making me fart too," she said, resting her bottom down on the grass, next to Daisy-Mae, who, looking down her nose, edged her perfect white, neatly clipped form a little away from the brown squat shape she now found plonked down next to her.

She'd have preferred Darcie not to be sat quite so

close; it wasn't that she disliked Darcie, but Daisy-Mae knew Darcie had a tendency to suddenly get up and violently shake herself, spraying dirt, old hair, and spittle far and wide. She didn't want to be near Darcie when that happened, no thank you. She most certainly didn't want traces of whatever Darcie shook out getting stuck in her poodle curls. So, she'd soon subtly manoeuvre herself away from the risk area. It would be rude to make it obvious, and as she really wanted some of that cake everyone was talking about, she'd best not chance upsetting Willow, who loved everyone, including farting, burping, messy Darcie.

"I really don't know what fun they have getting themselves so filthy," sniffed Daisy-Mae, looking across at the ever darkening coats of the two big dogs, still bouncing around in the distance. "All that yucky mud," she sighed, taking a step away from Darcie while looking down at her own neatly clipped, pristine white legs. She placed each of her tidy paws carefully on the greenest, driest spot of grass she could find.

She was always the same, Willow thought. Daisy-Mae hated her paws being wet, muddy, cold or dirty. Hated anyone else being any of those too. She was a little on the uptight side for a dog. She was also never seen out on days that weren't dry and clear, she couldn't risk a spot of dirt blotting her well preened appearance. Willow was mighty surprised to see she'd turned up to the party.

"Didn't think you'd come today," she said to her spotless friend, "thought it might be too messy for you?"

"It's your birthday, course I'd come," Daisy-Mae

replied, smoothly. "Wasn't going to miss having a piece of the famous birthday cake," she added, her tiny pink tongue delicately licking her neat black lips.

"Me neither," Darcie chimed in, releasing a smelly puff of trapped wind as she stood up. She was ready to hunt the cake.

"Shall we call them over for some cake?" Patsy asked Tom, who was stood chatting with Mrs Baker. At that moment, her dog Ollie was in a game of tag with a saucy black crow. Each time it touched down on the grass, Ollie – straining every Jack Russell sinew in his body – sprinted across the ground towards the bird. On, on, on he ran, his white body a blur of determination. Then, just as he was within a nose's reach, up flew the bird cackling with delight at the tease it had pulled off once again, before swooping down a short distance away from a panting Ollie.

"You'll be lucky Ollie," laughed Mrs Baker shaking her head. "Every morning that crow's here, larking about, teasing him. And he never gives up. It's the terrier in him, thinks he can catch anything that moves."

"Let's see if he'll come over for some of these," Patsy said as she put the last tray of biscuits out on the table. "Ollie, come! Come Ollie!"

Across the park, Ollie's ears twitched when he heard his name, but, his sharp, hazel eyes didn't leave the black bird and he didn't move an inch. This was a task requiring total concentration. The human on the end of the calling voice would have to wait. Which he was sure she would, she always did. Just one more go, he thought. This time, this flipping time, I'll get you.

I'm a terrier you know. You're just a crow. An annoying feathered creature. You're only a bird. Just because you can fly you think you can beat me at this? Well, I'm a dog, and not just any dog, I'm a Jack Russell terrier. And I can run. I can run and run. I can outrun anyone and one day, one day, I'll get you, I will. The thoughts were pelting around Ollie's mind and just as he was about to spring into action, the voice disturbed his concentration once again:

"Ohhhhh… llie, Ohhhhhh… llie. HERE! Ollie!"

Grrrr. Wait. Wait, I'm busy, Ollie thought, hearing his name again. Can't they see I'm busy?

"You're not still trying to get that bird are you?" Willow asked, as she ran up to Ollie's side. "Come on, they're finally getting the cake out. Leave the bird for later." She ran in a circle around her friend, and stopped still, right in front of him so he could no longer see the bird without having to peer around her body.

"Oh, ok, seeing as it's you," Ollie said, refocusing his gaze onto her, his concentration broken now anyway. Willow looked especially pretty stood in front of him, her black eyes sparkling. He'd always had a soft spot for her. Mmmm, yes, she was worth putting the bird aside for. And did she say cake? He was, now he thought about it, feeling quite famished.

8

> That is happiness; to be dissolved into
> something complete and great. When it
> comes to one, it comes as naturally as sleep.
>   Willa Cather, *My Ántonia*

Willow lay on the rug, stretched out on her side, her ribcage gently lifting and falling with each quiet, sleepy breath. She was exhausted after her party in the park and with her belly full of food, she was happily stuffed. There was no finer feeling than this, she thought. The food had been wolfed down by everybody, not a scrap had been left by the time her friends had finished and headed off home. Her birthday cake had been a huge success with everyone, and although Willow was happy to share it with her friends, a tiny slice of her thought it would have been perfectly fine if someone hadn't wanted their share, and she could have had a teeny bit more. But, as it was, she'd eaten so much that, as she drifted in and out of sleep on the rug, too sleepy to move into her bed, she wondered if she'd ever need to eat again.

"That went well, you pleased?" Tom asked Patsy as they sat together on the sofa.

"Really pleased. It's so lovely seeing the dogs all happy together. Just running about, being themselves. They're a lovely bunch."

"Did you see the state of Kai and Alfie? Head to tail covered in mud!" Tom said, shaking his head with a grin.

"And Daisy-Mae, she gobbled up that cake with less finesse than Darcie," chuckled Patsy. "It was all over her gorgeous white face by the time she'd finished, so funny!"

"Willow had a great time. All that running around and excitement's wiped her out," Tom said, looking down at Willow who was now snoring softly. "Dogs really don't ask for a lot do they?"

"Nope, they certainly don't. Friends, running around, playing with their mates, fresh air, a few games and good food. That's it, the simple, happy life of a dog!" Patsy laughed.

Then, her smile faded, "Did you hear what Di was saying about that little puppy Beebee, we met a couple of weeks ago?" Patsy lifted her feet to rest them on Tom's legs, and lay back against the pile of soft cushions.

"Just caught the end of it. She's been in the vet for something or other hasn't she?"

"Yep, been really ill apparently, nearly died. Some infection the vet thinks she must have had when they first bought her," Patsy sighed. "It's cost them a fortune getting her better, she's had days in the hospital, but thankfully she's pulled through. The kids have been really upset of course."

"Di said they'd got her from somewhere that wasn't nice, but as soon as they saw her, they couldn't leave her there, so bought her and took her home. Sad eh, but good for little Beebee," Tom said.

"Oh it is. It's horrible because the chances are, she probably came from a puppy farm or somewhere just as bad. Apparently when they tried to get in touch with the breeder and let them know the puppy was ill, they couldn't get hold of the woman. Disappeared. Must have been one of those dealers I've been reading about."

"Dealers?"

"They buy puppies from puppy farmers and sell them, pretending to be the breeder, they fool people all the time and make loads of money while they're at it. It's flipping awful. But, Beebee's going to be ok now, thank goodness… but… makes me worry about her mum and where she is, doesn't it you?" said Patsy.

"Yep, but what can you do?"

"The more I hear about all of this with puppies and puppy farming, and dealers, the more I know that getting Willow a new sister is something I'm going to do really carefully. I'm glad I've decided to adopt and not buy a puppy," Patsy said.

"Have to say, thinking about it and hearing about puppy Beebee today, I think you're right," Tom replied. "When you look at how happy Charlie is, and Darcie, both dogs who've been adopted, both really happy, no trouble at all. Well, if we ignore Darcie and her farting," he grinned.

"Yep. I know there's no need at all for me to buy a puppy to have a great new friend for us all, we'll definitely find the perfect dog to rehome. I'll take my time, I know for sure the right one'll come along," Patsy said.

"I don't think Willow's going to move again tonight do you? She's certainly not needing any supper by the look of her," Tom said, as Willow with a satisfied grunt, rolled over onto her back, legs in the air, showing off her plump, cake-filled tummy.

9

My doctrine is this, that if we see cruelty
or wrong that we have the power to
stop, and do nothing, we make ourselves
sharers in the guilt.

Anna Sewell, *Black Beauty*

I hear the Man in the barn but can't yet see him. I can't
see out of the space I'm trapped in, as the concrete walls
are high. Even when I was young, standing on my back
legs I was never able to see over the wall, however hard I
stretched and tried. All I can see are stark, concrete walls,
and if I look up, the tin roof of the barn high above me.
That's it. That's been my view for all these years.

Except, when the Man comes. Then, the cobweb
covered, rusting metal gate across the doorway to my pen
is pulled back and I can, if I'm quick, catch a glimpse of
a dirty, dusty pathway running outside my cell. On the
other side of the path is another row of identical heavy
iron gates and concrete pens. Prisons. The gate's never
open long, and mostly, I cower at the back of my prison,
away from the gate as I fear the Man might grab, or kick
me.

49

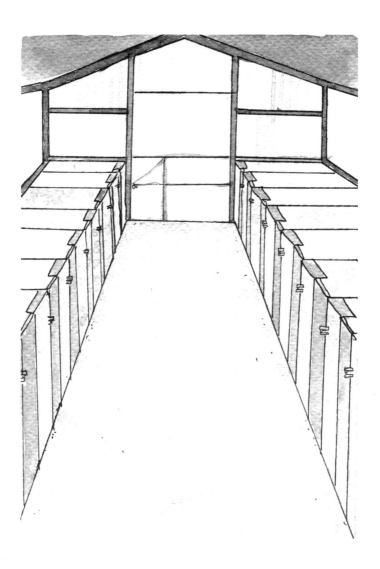

One awful day, when I was young and curious, I tried to peer out to see what lay beyond the walls that enclosed me. But the Man thought I was trying to escape and he slammed the gate shut, catching my leg between the gate and the concrete wall. Oh, the pain that shot through me in that split second as the heavy, steel gate crushed my leg. As I screamed, the Man looked down at me, shouting words of anger, his cruel face full of hate as he stomped off and left me.

I was in agony for ages afterwards but no help came. I cried for my mum who I hadn't seen for so long. I wanted her warm, soft body to huddle with. I craved her comforting cuddles. I remembered how sweet that feeling was when I was a puppy as I nuzzled in with her, among my brothers and sisters. As I lay on the cold, hard floor, I ached with sorrow and pain. Slowly, over many weeks my leg healed itself, but I've limped ever since. Not that I've had the chance to walk far in all these years. Just to and fro across the small square of my concrete cell.

What's that? I can hear the Man talking to someone, a woman. This is new, I've never heard her voice before. They're close by, must be standing at the pen next door to mine. Come to think about it, I haven't heard the dog in there for several days now. She used to be one of the noisier ones, sadly crying out, barking at all hours. In recent times, her voice has been weak, fading each day. I don't think the Man has been bringing her food as I've not heard him visit next door for some while now. The last time I heard anything, she was struggling to drag herself across her pen and that was days ago; there's been only chilling silence since.

Now what's this? I can hear the Man and woman speaking in sharper tones, my empty tummy flips over in fear. Suddenly, my neighbour's gate scrapes open, bringing a loud muffled gasp from the strange woman, followed by words I can't grasp. This is like nothing I've ever known. The atmosphere has changed, there's a frisson all around, but in the muddle I can't make out what I'm sensing. Despite my tired mind, through my weakness and fear I know something new is bristling on the air. Just as I'm struggling to gather enough strength to lift my nose higher, to prick my ears sharper…

BOOOFFF!

… the rusty, dusty gate is thrust open and there she stands. Owner of the voice.

I drop my eyes to the floor. She's standing there so big and tall, in her dark, smart uniform. I learnt long ago not to look directly at people. Looking at them brings trouble. Although my body is too weak to move much, I shrink back deeper into the corner of my pen, hoping to disappear from this unkind world, or at least from her. I try to hide my face, lowering my head, turning away from her, flattening my ears. I'm terrified of what might be about to happen. My heart's pounding, fear's rushing through my veins.

Above me, I can hear her speaking to the Man, who's replying in his gravelly, gruff voice. But hang on, he sounds different, his voice is quieter. It has none of its usual angry force. Out of the corner of my left eye I catch sight of his dirty black boot; I've seen and felt that hard, cruel toe enough times to know that it's his.

Why are they standing there? What are they saying

52

in a tight, choked exchange? Her voice is calm but firm. His? Well, it's the voice I've heard in all my tormented years, but now it seems to have lost its power. I'm confused and terror trembles deep inside me as none of this seems good. Maybe if I stay crouched, rock-still, they will go and leave me and all this will end.

Oh no, oh no, what's she doing now? She's moving into my pen, closer she comes, stepping carefully across the floor, picking her way past the piles of my poop that lie around. I stay rigid, trying not to breathe. My throat is tight with fear as she arrives at my side. Although I want to get away I can't risk it, and I try to stop myself trembling. If I make a wrong move, who knows what she'll do to me? Her smell fills my nose; it's like nothing I've ever smelt. It's kind of sweet, and as it enters my nose it lingers there; it's not unpleasant, in fact it has an appealing sugariness about it. This is weird and it's muddling my mind as I try to sort out all this newness.

I keep my eyes on the floor and look hard at one tiny speck of dirt among all the other filth there is around. If I keep looking at this small spot of black muck it will stop me from moving, my head from lifting and my eyes from seeing her. Down, down, I must keep my head down, my eyes fixed on the dirty spot there. It's right in front of my nose. I can do this, I can stay still and it'll all be over. She'll go. She'll leave me alone.

She's very close to me now, kneeling on the dirty floor, in the grubby spatter of sawdust that's been there forever. Out of the corner of my eye I can see her black trouser leg, it's within reaching distance of me. She could touch me if she stretched, just a little. I don't know what to do. I'm frantic inside, I can feel my heart thumping hard in my chest. Should I try to move away? No, I desperately must not move as I'm slow these days and she will surely grab me.

I can hear her breathing, it's slow and deep, and there's something else coming from her. I don't think they're words, although it is a whispering sound I hear. No, she's not speaking, at least they're not words that I know. Or even sounds which I've heard before. Like her unusual smell, these noises are all new. It's a soft murmuring that gently enters my muck-filled, smelly ears which have known only terrible sounds of terror and cruelty. This noise soothes my painful, infected ears.

I'm mighty confused, scared, and finding it hard to keep my gaze fixed on the dark spot of dirt. Where is the Man? I dare not lift my head to see if he's still standing there, or if he's with her, here close in my pen somewhere. But I can't stay like this for much longer. My back and hips and knees are burning with pain. I need to shift position, just a little, but if I move, what will she do?

OUCH!

OUCH!

Oh no!

NO!

No, no, this is terrifying. She has me in her hands. She's got hold of me. She made a grab and stood up straight with me clasped in her arms and I'm now rising into the air. High up, up, higher I go in her arms. What on earth's happening? She's holding me close to her chest. I'm so scared I can't breathe. This is terrible.

Awful. Scary. My leg's hurting, my hip is screaming with pain and she has me clasped in her arms so tight that I'm sure I will snap. Where is she taking me?

10

I don't understand it any more than you do, but one thing I've learned is that you don't have to understand things for them to be.

Madeleine L'Engle, *A Wrinkle In Time*

"Your new sister's going to be a very special dog, and you're going to be a great friend for her. She's a dog no one's ever loved," Patsy whispered into Willow's grey, fluffy ear late one morning as they were cuddling on the sofa. With a little wriggle Willow slid down against Patsy's arm, turned onto her back and, with a deep sigh rested her head back against the sofa's armrest. That was better, now she was perfectly comfy.

"We'll put that right won't we?" Patsy said, running her fingers through Willow's white tummy fluff. "We'll show her what it's like to be loved and spoilt rotten," she smiled, bending her head to blow a muffled raspberry on Willow's soft, round belly.

Willow loved these lazy mornings, and hearing Patsy talk about her new sister made this an extra special one. It wasn't long after her birthday, and Patsy had been busy looking into adopting a dog. Each day she'd been scouring the internet, speaking on the phone and becoming, in Willow's opinion, a tad obsessed. At least all the research that was done assured Willow that whoever was coming into their lives had been thoroughly thought about, and well prepared for. Today was an important day. It was the day she was going to hear all about the dog Patsy had found, who was to be her new sister, as someone from the rescue charity was coming to talk to Patsy.

Willow really liked the idea of a sister, she'd been thinking about it a lot since her birthday, with plans and thoughts buzzing in and out of her head for days. For a start, she couldn't wait to share all her favourite walks. There were so many good places Willow planned on sharing, a million great routes for sniffing and running, it was going to be exciting to explore together. Then there were her toys. She turned her head a little on the armrest and looked over at her overflowing, wicker toy basket that sat under the window. Yes, she could and would let her new sister play with most of her toys, after all she had plenty to share. Although, as she spotted poking out of the top of the basket the orange leg of her special, squishy octopus, she wondered if she might save that one, just that particular toy for herself; it really was her favourite. Willow wasn't quite sure if she could bear to share it with anyone, not even her brand new sister.

As Patsy stroked her tummy, Willow looked up at the ceiling and thought about what Patsy had been discovering over recent weeks. On many afternoons, Willow had sat at her feet while Patsy was tapping away on her computer, trawling for information. Sometimes she'd be upset at something on the screen, and Willow would snuggle onto her feet to offer comfort. It always worked, as one of Patsy's hands would slide down and stroke Willow's ears, letting her know she was fine. Sometimes she'd say what she'd found: she told Willow of dogs in sheds, in barns, being kept for years in the dark; poorly puppies with their sick mums and dads being rescued and taken to new lives, safe in the arms of their rescuers.

Some days it all got too upsetting and up from her desk Patsy would jump, grab Willow's lead, and out they'd go for a brisk walk and fresh air. As she strode along with Willow, taking deep breaths it cleared her head to be outdoors walking. Willow didn't mind, she was always keen to go for a walk so long as it wasn't raining. She couldn't imagine how dogs in puppy farms could live without walking, never having the chance to explore or run. It pained her to ponder how unhappy they must be.

Then not long ago, Patsy had found a small charity that rescued dogs from puppy farms. Willow had listened intently while Patsy told Tom, her voice full of barely contained excitement; she'd said the charity took any dogs they could from the puppy farms and found new families for them to go and live with. They needed families. They needed people like Patsy. She'd lost no time making contact with the charity. They'd asked her lots of questions and told Patsy that her and Willow sounded like a great new family for one of their special dogs to join. And that was how today had become the special day, as arrangements were made for someone called Val from the charity to visit, and tell them all about the dogs the charity rescued, in particular the dog who Patsy hoped would become Willow's new sister.

"Gosh, look at the time, we'd better get moving," Patsy patted Willow, who turned herself over and jumped off the sofa in one smooth movement.

"Val's coming about 12, so just time to get a quick walk in before she arrives. It's exciting, we'll hear all about our new friend."

11

She who saves a single soul, saves the universe.

Lewis Carroll,
Alice's Adventures in Wonderland

We're in my concrete cell, the dusty air of the barn is thick in my nostrils. She's standing with me in her arms. Her warm, strong arms. And I'm petrified. I'm desperately trying to hold my head still and look straight ahead. I must not look at her.

Must not look.

I can hear and feel her breathing above my head. It's calm and steady, and her warm, sweet scented breath is softly brushing the top of my head. Her arms are cradling my weak body with a hold that's not as tight as I thought it was a second or two ago. It's secure but not painful. I just thought it would hurt when she lifted me off the cold floor and into her arms. But no, it doesn't, although I'm still scared as hell. My ribs press against her arms as I let out my own tight breath, just a tiny bit. A release of small breath and slight movement into the soft cushion of her arms.

My head's spinning now as she turns slowly, moving towards the open gate of my pen. I can't see or hear the Man. I'm not really able to see much as I must keep my head still; I daren't move it to see where he is. I'm safest when I don't move.

Now where is she taking me? Her body bumps and squashes against mine as she carries me out of the pen, along the dingy path. I think I can see a light at the end, far in the distance through the murky barn, yes, there's a definite blur of light. She's talking to me as she walks towards the growing brightness; I'm certain she's speaking to me but I can't understand anything. My head is a swirl of confusion. The sounds in the barn are different. There are other voices, ones I've never heard before and coming towards us is another person, a man I think but I can't see him clearly. I've been used to the darkness for so long, the new light's making my eyes sting.

Blink, blink, now he's closer, I can see he's also wearing a dark uniform. He stands in front of us and we stop. He speaks quietly to the woman and looks down at me, they're talking above my head and I sense they're cross. But, not with me. I can't say how I know this, but I know for certain that it's not me they're angry with. They pity me, I sense their sad, heavy hearts full of pity… for me.

The new man looks closely at me, he bends his face close to mine, and I can see him for the first time. I let myself for a flash of a second look at him. His bearded face is kind; he whispers something to me and I feel his gentle touch on my shoulder. And it terrifies me.

12

You're mad, bonkers, completely off your head. But I'll tell you a secret. All the best people are.

Lewis Carroll,
Alice's Adventures in Wonderland

After a brisk walk across the Downs, shortly after they got back to the house, and Patsy had whizzed around doing last minute tidying, there was a sharp tap-tap on the door knocker. Willow bounded through the hallway, skidding to a halt as she reached the front door, plonked her bottom neatly on the mat, and looked keenly up at Patsy, waiting for her to open the door.

"Now be your best, sweetie" Patsy smiled down at her, opening the door.

On the doorstep stood Val, a small, silver haired lady wearing a neat pink jacket, sky blue jumper, smart black trousers and a huge smile. Willow, sitting on the doormat at Patsy's feet, searched Val's face, scanning every tiny detail, picking up information, trying to look into her eyes which seemed to have disappeared into smiling crinkles.

"Hi, Val I presume?" Patsy smiled, reaching out her hand which Val took warmly in both of hers as she stepped into the hallway.

"Oh yes, yes, so pleased to come and meet you both," Val smiled, slowly bending down on one knee to be closer to Willow's level, turning her head slightly away and offering the back of her hand, for Willow to sniff and inspect.

"And you must be Willow, I've heard lots of good things about you, little darling," she cooed, as Willow nuzzled her hand, pushing her fluffy grey head up underneath it for a more hearty stroke. She could tell this new person was someone she was going to like very much indeed, everything felt, and smelt good about Val.

"Aren't you a gorgeous girl?" Val cupped Willow's bristly chin in both her small, brown speckled hands, gently rubbing her fingers through Willow's freshly washed and brushed, bushy white beard.

Oh yes, that had been the only blot on Willow's day yesterday. Patsy had decided that, as Val was coming to talk about her new sister, she needed a bath and beard wash and this was never on Willow's long list of fun things to do. She could never understand why, out of the blue, suddenly Patsy felt the need to plop her in the bath tub, scrub and shampoo her with sweetly smelling gooey stuff, and then rinse it all off again. She hated the warm water trickling down her face, through her beard, while up and down her body and legs Patsy moved the shower spray, until she decided it had been going on for long enough.

Why, oh, why was all that annoying water needed?

Willow wondered this every single bath-time as she did her best to stand still and not wriggle about. Standing still was essential, but hard. She found that if she lost concentration and shook herself in the middle of the rinsing off, spraying water all over the bathroom walls, the showering would go on even longer, prolonging the ordeal, so she did her absolute best to stand still. But this was not easy when the water was running down through her ears, making them soggy and heavy, flattening them to the side of her head; and her eyebrows, dripping wet, all over her eyes so she couldn't see a thing except a wet curtain of her own fur. Baths were definitely a great annoyance in Willow's life.

Then, suddenly, it would be over, Patsy turned off the taps, and it was done. Shampooed, rinsed, finished. Just like that! But, and this Willow could never understand, to make it seem even more of a pointless ordeal, Patsy always then set about briskly drying her. Why, Willow wondered did she get her all wet in the first place? And there was an even odder thing, Patsy never let Willow do what she really wanted, something that she was rather good at doing, and which she loved the most. Which was to give herself a violent head to tail shake, followed by a bonkers run around the house drying her face on the carpets and edges of the sofas. Then, and this was the very best bit, she'd take a flying leap up onto Patsy's bed to roll herself over and over right in the middle of it. The big expanse of crisp, white clean duvet was the perfect drying spot. The problem was, Patsy didn't seem to agree and most bath days she insisted on wrapping Willow up in a big, warm, fluffy towel, cuddling her tightly to her chest and rubbing dry Willow's dripping wet, furry body. Although Willow loved the cuddle, it seemed a daft way to end what was, from start to finish, a tedious and not enjoyable pastime. The only sliver of fun Willow had ever winkled out of having a bath was the boisterous post-bath drying run around the house and up and over the furniture. That always felt ridiculously good.

Never mind, yesterday's bath was the last thing on Willow's mind as she sat on the doormat, close to Val's bent knee and soaked up the generous supply of gentle strokes. Val really was an excellent stroker, Willow thought, as she felt a pair of confident hands moving slowly, expertly along her shoulders and down her back. Clearly here was a person who knew how to make a dog happy Willow decided, as her head drooped lower and lower and she couldn't resist sliding down and flopping over onto her back, offering up her tummy to Val's magical hands.

"Come on Willow, I think that's enough soppy girl for now," Patsy laughed, as Val gave Willow's tummy a final, gentle pat as she stood up and followed Patsy through to the kitchen where tea and lemon drizzle cake were waiting. Willow pulled herself quickly round and up onto her four paws, and trotted alongside Val, feeling happily stroked, wagging her fluffy tail as she went. She was eager to snaffle a taste of cake if she could, as Val seemed a softie worth trying her cake-begging skills out on. And of course, she wanted to hear more about her new sister.

"Willow's a little sweetheart," Val smiled, as she sat herself at the kitchen table, nodding as Patsy offered her tea.

"Oh she is, really she's such a lovely dog," Patsy said, as she put the white china mug of tea on the table in front of her guest. "I'm sure she's going to love having a new sister, but, I want to be really sure it's the right thing for us all."

"Of course, you're doing exactly the right thing here, taking your time, thinking it through, and this home visit's really helpful for all of us," Val glanced over at Willow who was sat in her bed, patiently waiting for the cake to be cut. "It's important you and I are both happy with everything, and you're clear about what's ahead, and what help you might need and you know you can always phone me and ask for that," Val looked deeply into Patsy's eyes, slightly raising her eyebrows as she made certain Patsy understood the offer of help was there.

"Thanks, I'm hoping we won't need to bother you much, but that's great to know," Patsy nodded, taking a sip of tea.

"Ok, let me tell you all about Maya", Val said.

13

Genuinely good people are like that.
The sun shines out of them. They warm
you right through.

Michael Morpurgo,
Alone on a Wide Wide Sea

I'm awake, not knowing where I am for a few terrifying
seconds. My mind grapples with the flood of confusing
messages my body is sending me: soft bed, clean blanket,
no sawdust, thick carpet, sweet smells, no dogs crying
or barking, no hunger, no concrete walls, soft lights,
warm glow from the fire burning in the grate. And her.
Sitting there. Now I remember what's happened, as
my brain sorts through the muddling blur and I relax
as I remember her. The silver-haired, quietly spoken
human, with soft, freckled hands, who brought me here
a few days ago is sitting there, in an armchair, across the
room. She's watching me, but pretending she's not, with
a book in her hands. Her eyes are lowered but I know
she's looking at me.

My mind is racing with all that's happened to me. It
comes back in a rush of images and remembered strange

sounds and smells. Everything's changed. Absolutely everything is different in my world.

After being carried out of the barn by the woman in uniform, I was put with a few other dogs into a van and taken on a terrifying journey. This was the first time for all of us that we were away from the confinement of the barn and every minute in the van terrified us. Some of the dogs pooped themselves in fear, others were sick and by the time we reached our destination the inside of the van smelt almost as bad as the barn where we'd spent our lives. The next few hours remain a foggy fuddle in my mind, memories of being handled by strange people, given fresh food and water and a bath; this was the first time in my life that I'd felt warm water on my skin, not a cold blast from a hose. Although it was frightening, it was oddly good being wet and warm, not cold and soggy.

I remember spending a while, possibly a few days, I'm not sure as I had no way to judge time, in a small, warm kennel where there was a soft squashy bed. I sniffed it all over, taking in the queer smell of this curious object, and almost stepped into it to see what it would feel like to lie down and be enveloped in comfort; but in the end, I was too scared to dare and lay instead on the hard floor as that's what I'm used to.

It was quiet and warm in the kennel. Strange and unsettling. There was a clean water bowl, full to the brim with crystal clear water. But, I only risked taking the tiniest sip of its refreshing deliciousness, not trusting that it would be refilled if I emptied it. Years of knowing the misery of thirst means I take nothing for granted.

She's still watching me, while pretending to read her book,

and I'm trying not to catch her eye, keeping my head low on this soft, warm bed.

I spent those first befuddling days with another dog, a small apricot poodle. We didn't know each other until we met in the shelter, but she'd come on the same journey with me out of the puppy farm. She was younger than me, and not as thin, nor as weak and worn out. But, like me, she was petrified of the strangeness surrounding us. We huddled together for comfort, hoping that whatever was going on it was better than where we'd come from. And it was, we sensed it was, but weren't able to overcome our fears.

The people around in those first days out of the puppy farm are in my head now as a jumble of odd figures and sounds. I was bombarded by oddness. Nothing was familiar and I can't remember any single human as an individual, instead they've all merged into a memory of quiet, gentle kindness. They smelt good too, I do recall that: a new smell, the odour of love mingling with kindness. When they came to the kennel, they whispered, moving silently and slowly; they never grabbed us, or hurried to do anything. It was weird and I wrestled with the niceness on offer, as nastiness is all I've known. I resisted the confusing feelings of comfort that were creeping into me, bizarrely at times wanting to be back in my familiar concrete pen. But, in among the many mindboggling moments, an itsy-bitsy part of me wanted the kindness that was swooshing around to wash over my mind and body and make everything better. I didn't want to resist it; I wanted to go to sleep, wake up and no longer feel frightened. But I couldn't quite give in and let that happen.

Then suddenly, out of the blue I was on another journey with the lady who is now sat over there, in the armchair by the fire. One day she came to the shelter with another lady, they seemed to be friends. Both quietly sat on the clean, grey tiled floor of the kennel, as me and Poodle huddled together in our bed. The two women didn't do much, they chatted softly to each other, and at times to us, although I wasn't at all sure what they were saying. The unusual soft tones of human voices were taking some getting used to, without the dreaded, but familiar violence of the Man attached.

After a while, the ladies seemed to make a decision and that was it: Poodle went with the other one and I came here; so here I am, in a quiet house with a strange, kind lady called Val.

14

> I've got a new friend, all right. But what
> a gamble friendship is!
>
> E.B. White, *Charlotte's Web*

"Hey, hey sweetie," Willow heard Patsy calling as if from another world. "Wakey wakey!"

She opened her eyes and looked straight into Patsy's blue ones. The dream was over, which was a shame as she'd been right in the middle of a rollicking chase game in the fantasy world of a new best friend, who also happened to be her sister. And the fantasy was about to become reality, or so she hoped.

Willow got out of her bed, stretched her paws out in front of her as far as they would go, dropped her shoulders to the ground, lifted her grey bottom in the air and stretched for a few seconds; then stretched her back a bit more before pulling her weight up onto her shoulders and pushing her neck forwards to its farthest point, which had the elastic effect of lifting her back legs up onto the tips of her toes. Then she snapped herself back together with a vigorous shake, zippy enough to lift her, just for a second, off the bedroom carpet before landing back down and staring up at Patsy.

"Better? Awake now?" Patsy smiled down at her from the bed where she was sat up, her red hair wild and messy against the pile of white pillows. "Remember what's happening today?"

Of course Willow remembered! It was the only thing she'd been thinking about since she'd found out about it yesterday. Well, that plus last night's delicious chicken dinner. She was so excited she could burst, but shook herself again instead.

"It's exciting isn't it?" Patsy said, patting the white duvet beside her to invite Willow up for their first cuddle of the morning. Willow leapt up and tucked herself tightly into Patsy's warm embrace, thinking of the day ahead.

She was going to meet her new sister, Maya. It had all been arranged with Val: they were to drive to her cottage where Maya was being fostered with Val and her other dogs. She'd been there for a few weeks, being cared for, and learning how to live in a home, which was an alien world for Maya. Willow didn't know many details, but she understood that her sister had been saved from somewhere terrible; the puppy farm sounded like a different planet compared to the cosy home shared by Patsy and Willow. A place where there was always a choice of plush beds to settle into, one in each room of the house; whereas her sister had lived on nothing but sawdust and concrete. In one of their many telephone chats following her first visit to them, Val had warned Patsy that the damaged and scared dog who was going to be Willow's sister, may not trust that her new bed with them was hers to lie in and relax upon; in fact, she might not even know how to relax at all for a good while.

However hard Willow tried to bend her mind to this curious and disturbing thought, she couldn't untangle the confusion it created in her: how could a dog see a comfy bed and not know she could just clamber in and enjoy it? How sad and mixed up poor Maya must be, not to know the simplest thing: that a snug bed equals a comfy nest. Her sister was scared of many things in her new world outside of the puppy farm, and she would need a lot of help to learn how to live happily. Willow also thought she'd need loads of sisterly love, which was fine, as she had oodles to offer; Willow was overflowing with it and she hadn't even met Maya.

If all went well today, Patsy and Val would sort out the details, and in a few days time her sister would be here and they'd begin their new life together. Willow itched with excited impatience. But, there was a shadow of worry which flickered from time to time: was it possible that a dog could be too scared to enjoy having a new sister like her? What if Maya's fears were too much and Willow couldn't find ways to help her? Or, and this was a dreadful thought, what if Maya didn't like Willow? No, no, that last worry Willow pushed aside, she was being silly, everyone liked her, it was unimaginable that her new sister wouldn't. Wasn't it?

"Come on, let's get ready. Breakfast?" Patsy threw back the bed covers and Willow leapt off the bed, landing expertly on the thick bedroom carpet.

A couple of hours later and Patsy and Willow were

speeding through the countryside in the car, to Val's house, which was in the middle of nowhere. Willow enjoyed car rides, she found the scenes swishing past the windows thrilling, and a car journey nearly always had something good at the end of it. Like a beach walk, or meeting up with friends she hadn't seen for a while. Or, like today, visiting Val and Maya. There were occasional blips, like the morning Patsy had bundled her into the car and she'd found herself spending the day at the vet with all kinds of weird things going on. Willow remembered the word 'spay' being mentioned a few times, but that was a journey and a day that Willow liked to forget, and seeing as Patsy had spoilt her silly for a few days afterwards, she'd quickly forgiven her – and almost forgotten it.

"OK! We're here!" Patsy said, as she pulled the car into the gravelled driveway of a small, rose-coloured cottage. As she turned off the car engine, the front door of the cottage opened, and out through the low doorway stepped a smiling Val. With her came three dogs trotting at her feet, one a small, light-brown terrier, barking loudly at the visitors.

"Don't mind Wilson," Val shook her head, pointing at the noisy, barky dog. "He thinks every visitor needs a loud hello from him. For a small dog, he makes quite a racket. He'll stop yattering in a mo, once he knows we're all ok here."

Patsy smiled over her shoulder at Val as she turned to release Willow from her car harness. "Oh don't worry, Willow's exactly the same if the mood grabs her. She loves a good welcome bark."

As Willow jumped from the car and together they crunched over the gravel towards Val, the other two dogs, one brown, the other white, trotted over to inspect the strangers while Wilson stayed close to Val's feet.

"You've a lot to say for yourself, little man," Patsy smiled down at Wilson, who was almost quietening down, just adding a final, squeaky, half-hearted woof, as he peered closely at the visitors from the safety of Val's side.

"He does, always. And he's totally harmless. He's been out the puppy farm now a good few years. Sadly he's losing his eyesight. Not that it seems to bother him much, but, sad all the same," Val said, bending down and stroking the brown, wiry coated shoulder of a now quiet Wilson.

"Gosh that *is* sad. Nothing that can be done?"

"Nope, nothing at all," Val said, sadness passing across her normally happy face as she led them through the open front door into the cottage's small hallway. All the dogs trotted in behind her, Wilson squeezing his slim body through, to be in front.

"Dreadful," Patsy said, glancing around, discretely looking for any hint of where Maya might be.

"Puppy farms, terrible business. But, enough of the sadness. Shall we go and meet Maya?"

"Oh yes, please, yes… have to say we're a bit excited aren't we Willow? Patsy looked back at Willow who was behind her, still by the front door, having a sniff of the white dog's bottom, but when she heard her name, she looked up and trotted forward.

"OK, Maya, Maya, darling, it's only me," Val softly called, opening the door into a small, primrose-yellow living room with low beams and a fire burning in the grate, "here, meet your new sister, Willow."

15

I am not afraid of storms, for I am
learning how to sail my ship.
Louise May Alcott, *Little Women*

Patsy and Willow followed Val into the snug, warm
room. Weak sunlight streamed through a bay window
on the front wall, under which on the thick carpet was
a dog bed; and there, tucked into the corner of the big
squashy tweed cushion, was Maya. She sat alert, closely
watching the visitors as they entered the room. When
she spotted Willow, Maya straightened herself, lifting her
nose with a slight twitch of curiosity; their eyes locked
and as Willow toddled over to say hello, Maya stood up
in the bed, leaning forwards to greet her visitor. Their
black wet noses touched for the first time.

"Aww, how sweet," Patsy whispered to Val as they
sat down on the sofa to watch the dogs go through
their greeting. The ritual, practiced the same by dogs
the world over, involved a thorough inspection of each
other's face and a lot of sniffing of ears and eyes before
moving round to bottoms. As all dogs are, both Maya
and Willow were fascinated by the odours of each other

and once a full check had been done, they were happy. Maya moved back into the corner of the bed, farthest from the human visitors as Willow turned back to them, her shining black eyes searching out Patsy's.

"So, what do you think?" Patsy asked, Willow's wagging tail giving all the answer she needed.

"We'll let the others in now," Val stood up, to open the living room door.

"I can see they've done this before!" Patsy said, as Wilson and the other two dogs got up off a small brown bed that was just outside the door, where they'd been waiting patiently.

"Oh yes, they know the routine with my foster dogs and their visitors, they give them the space they need, we're all well trained here," Patsy chuckled. "Silly me, I didn't introduce you all properly though. That's what happens when Wilson does his noisy thing, I end up forgetting introductions!" Val picked up the tiny white dog, planting a kiss on her head. "This is Isla. She's our old lady, must be about twelve or thirteen now, aren't you sweetie? She's been with me now for... gosh let me think... yes, must be quite a few years, at least ten. Going a bit deaf, but open the biscuit tin and she soon hears that!" Val put Isla down on the bed beside Maya who had her eyes on Val the whole time.

"And that's Wilf, he's much younger." As he heard his name, Wilf padded across the soft carpet towards Val. "Didn't have a great start in life... was kept outside on a chain till he was rescued. He was in a sorry old state when he came here, but, you wouldn't know it now. Not when you see him running across the fields chasing rabbits," Val stroked Wilf's sleek brown head as he gazed up at her with his unusual mustard coloured eyes full of love. "He's always great with my foster dogs, he helps them settle in here, in no time. There's a quiet confidence about you Wilf isn't there, that helps them relax."

With that, Wilf ambled across the room to the bed, where Isla shifted herself to make room for him and tucked her small white, elderly body into the corner as he lay himself down, close to, but in front of Isla and Maya. After a couple of seconds, Maya slumped gently down, resting her head across his back, keeping her wary eyes on the rest of the room.. The warmth of the room was making Isla sleepy and with half closed eyes, a gentle snore was soon heard coming from her. Willow took one look at the peaceful scene and moved over to the bed, giving each of the dogs' noses a quick sniff before turning, and with a sigh she flopped down on the carpet beside the bed. After looking up at Patsy and Val, her eyes moved down to Wilson who was now sat up on Val's lap enjoying a thoroughly pleasant stroking, no hint remaining of his earlier, noisy agitation at the visitors' arrival.

"Well I think we can safely say there's no problems here!" Val said, a broad smile spreading across her face.

"They're so peaceful," Patsy agreed. "I didn't think I needed to worry that Willow would get on with Maya, she's always a friendly girl, but to see them both here, right now, looking so at home together is lovely. And a relief, I'll admit, you never quite know do you?"

"Not at all, you hear all sorts of stories, not all with happy endings," sighed Val. "It's always best to check the dogs do get along before committing, but really, it's so rare any of my foster dogs don't get on with others… in fact I don't ever remember one not," she paused, as Wilson stood up and gave himself a good shaking before settling himself back in the centre of Val's soft lap, which was now covered with a thin dusting of light-brown dog hairs. "Better?" she smiled, tickling Wilson's bristly chin.

"Do you think it's because they've been through such rough times, they can see the good times coming, and are happy to get on with their new friends when they get the chance?" Patsy asked.

"Quite possibly, yes. Dogs are amazing, we could learn a lot from them and how they move on. Right, fancy a potter round the garden?"

16

If we're in each other's dreams, we can be together all the time.

A.A. Milne, *Winnie The Pooh*

That night I dreamed I was back in the puppy farm with my babies, my first litter of sweet, innocent puppies. In the dark and dusty barn we huddled together on the cold concrete floor, while in my dream I whispered to them that they would soon be leaving on a big adventure. They would be travelling out of the barn and into a whole new world, where kind humans and nice dogs were waiting for them.

My first born, a beautiful grey girl, whimpered and cried, full of fears saying she was too scared to be away from me and terrified of what lay ahead. I dreamt I licked her face, assuring her she must be brave, as the world outside the barn was a much kinder place. It was where she was meant to go, to live, to love and be loved; not to stay stuck in the dark, dirt and misery of the puppy farm. As my tongue worked its soothing way over her body, she began to calm and settle, and into her ear I dreamily whispered that she'd soon find herself in a warm safe home, and her life would be full of nice things. There'd be soft beds and plump cushions, scrumptious food and crystal clear water in her bowl at all times. She'd never feel too hot or too cold, or hungry or thirsty, and if she did, the humans she lived with would take care of her and make everything all right. She'd have toys and games, and friends to play with; there would be fun and laughter, and happiness all around. But, if she stayed with me in the barn, there were only dark and cruel days ahead. It was not the place a dog should be.

I dreamt I was gifted the luxury of time to prepare all my babies for their new lives in this way, as we shared our last night together, their happy young hearts throbbing and thrilled with excitement at the wonders that lay ahead. And then I woke, and my years of misery came crashing back; all the happiness I'd been robbed of, replaced by days of tragic sadness that marked my life. But, as I lay awake in the quiet calm of Val's cottage, coddled amid the comforting warmth of Isla, Wilson and Wilf, I resolved to put the sadness behind me, and to grasp the happy peace that was almost within reach. The joy that shone from beautiful Willow, inspired me. She would show me the way towards being happy. Although I was scared, and worried about the unknown path ahead, I knew I wanted more than anything in the world to be happy, and loved like Willow.

17

> The sun was rising behind her now; she could feel the heat on her back, and it gave her courage.
>
> William Goldman, *The Princess Bride*

A few days after collecting Maya from Val's to start her new life, Patsy sat with Maya in Kettlecroft Park, watching Willow chase the crow with Ollie. The bird, as usual was enjoying himself in his crow-like way tormenting the two determined dogs by landing within feet of them, and cawing loudly before flying off with a feathery flourish, as they raced in closer.

Alongside Patsy on the wooden bench sat Mrs Baker, keeping an eye on Ollie and his antics as she did every morning, come rain or shine. Patsy's red hair shone bright in the morning sun.

"At last it feels like spring's arrived… did you see the daffodils are out over by the beech trees?" Mrs Baker said, waving her walking stick towards the bright flash of yellow beyond where Willow and Ollie were stalking the black feathered tease.

"Beautiful aren't they?" Patsy replied. She always

loved springtime with its new beginnings and brighter days. Perfect timing for Maya's new life to get underway.

"So, how's she doing? Have heard a lot about her from everyone," Mrs Baker said, nodding down at Maya who sat at their feet, unmoving on the grass, her eyes fixed on Ollie and Willow a couple of hundred meters in front of her. Caught in the spring sunshine her grey head appeared flecked with shining strands of polished silver.

"She's doing good thanks," Patsy replied, giving the back of Maya's neck a gentle stroke, being careful not to startle her. "Really good, considering what she's been through in her life. Little things like this, just touching her can spook her, she's so unused to humans, or at least humans being nice to her. We do everything very slowly at the moment."

"Not letting her off lead yet?"

"No, no, too risky just yet, I've got to be certain she's not going to bolt off if something scares her," Patsy replied, edging along the bench to be a little closer to Maya. "We're working on basics at home, getting her used to me calling her. She's very greedy, loves her food, which is making things easy as I can tempt her, and treat her with tasty titbits."

"Oooooh, knowing how you like to bake, and all the yummy things you bring out here for us all, I bet she's loving her new home… must seem like she's in Paradise compared to the hell she's come from!" Mrs Baker chuckled.

Patsy smiled, "Yep, it does seem to be helping her trust me. We're all happy: me, I have a good reason to bake; Willow, she's getting all her favourites, and Maya… well… we can only hope Maya's starting to know what happiness is."

"And the two of them are getting along ok?"

"Oh yes, perfectly… couldn't have hoped for better, Willow's a great teacher, and Maya's brilliant at copying her so that's helping loads. Willow's also very happy to have a new friend," Patsy said, thinking how at ease Willow and Maya were together. From the moment Maya entered the house, Willow embraced the role of big sister, happily showing her the household routines and helping Maya to get through each day. Patsy marvelled at the way Maya looked to her sister for comfort, cautiously following everything that Willow did. Many things frightened Maya, like going up and down the stairs which had taken her a few days

to master, but eventually, she had got the hang of it with Willow's help. Patsy was sure, slowly, day by day, Maya's fears were fading.

"Puppy farm dogs get along with other dogs, it's all they've ever known in their lives. It's humans that scare them, sad they have to get used to us," Patsy said.

Wherever Willow was, Patsy knew Maya would be, whether they were pottering side by side in the garden, or hovering in the kitchen waiting for dinner. Patsy knew that Maya was learning far more from her sister, than she ever would from Patsy. The relationship between the dogs was blossoming by the day and it was wonderful to see.

"Makes my blood boil hearing how cruel these places are," Mrs Baker said. "How anyone can treat dogs like it's beyond me, so much for man's best friend!" she said shaking her head.

"Agree, it's really horrible. But, that's all behind this little one at least," Patsy smiled, as Maya shifted position to lay her head on her paws, eyes still on her sister and Ollie in the distance.

"Makes you wonder what she's thinking, doesn't it? You wondering what your sister and my daft boy Ollie are doing over there chasing that flippin' bird? Wonder myself at times!" chuckled Mrs Baker.

"I know, she could be wanting to join in, to run, to feel the fun of the chase... I wonder. She's never done it, I know that for sure. Being cooped up in a tiny pen her whole life and only now being strong enough to get out and about, I wonder if she's itching to run. Or, she might just be completely bewildered by it all, who knows?" Patsy shrugged, reaching down once more to give Maya a reassuring stroke.

"Well, I'm sure whatever she's thinking, you and Willow are doing a grand job. She couldn't have found herself a better home. Brrrr, there's still a nip in the air," Mrs Baker buttoned her coat and tightened her scarf as a gust of wind rustled across the park. "Right! We'd better be off, things to do, see you again," and with that Mrs Baker was up off the bench and across the grass calling Ollie, who appeared not to hear her as he ran in the opposite direction.

"That's a Jack Russell for you," Patsy smiled, as Mrs Baker turned and pointed her stick, shaking her head with a smile at Ollie. Nothing changed, Ollie did his own thing and Mrs Baker loved him all the same.

Shortly afterwards, with Willow happily tired from her romping about, Patsy, Maya and Willow made their way home along the footpath. What must Maya have been thinking? Patsy wondered, seeing her sister and Ollie running helter-skelter around the park. Did she have any sense running might be fun? Bizarre that a dog would have to learn to enjoy something so basic, but this was how it was. Were you watching your sister in a state of utter bewilderment? Patsy puzzled. Although it was impossible to know what Maya's mind was juggling with, as her life had been so far from a normal dog's, it would be a wonder if she wasn't bamboozled by every moment in each new day.

Patsy remembered Val's parting words when she'd brought Maya home, "She'll need you to take things slowly. She's still a very frightened girl, finding her feet in a scary new world… she's raw, she has everything to discover about living with humans. Be patient. And trust Willow to show her the way."

Patsy planned on doing just that, and had the perfect place in mind for the next stage in Maya's journey.

18

The moment you doubt whether you can fly, you cease for ever to be able to do it.

J.M. Barrie, *Peter Pan*

The morning sun sparkled across the sea. The sand was strewn with tangles of brown and green seaweed brought in and left behind by the tide. A young man, in a striped tee shirt and shorts was hard at work with a stiff broom scrubbing the wooden decking in front of a row of colourful beach huts.

"There he is," Tom said, walking with Willow beside him across the sand towards the man. Patsy followed with Maya.

"Hiya mate," the man said, as he stopped what he was doing, dropped his broom and clasped Tom in a huge hug.

"It's been too long!" Tom grinned, as they stepped back from each other, broad smiles on both men's faces.

"Really has, but you're here now."

"Yep, better late than never! Patsy meet Dave, Dave meet Patsy," Tom said, flourishing his arms in a silly way.

"Nice to meet you at long last, heard all about you," Dave smiled at Patsy who shook his outstretched hand warmly.

"Likewise," she said, glancing down at Maya who stood behind her legs. Maya's tail was tucked in, her head hung low, her black eyes were cast down; she was anxious. She must be worried about the stranger or the new environment, or both, thought Patsy with a little tug of sadness, as she realised the growing confidence that Maya showed at home was still fragile.

"And who are these beauties?" Dave asked, kneeling down to greet the dogs. Willow pushed forward to stand in front of Maya, eager to say hello to this new man who was clearly a friend of Tom and Patsy's, and to let Maya know she was checking him out for them both and her sister needn't fret.

"That's Willow... think she likes you," Tom smiled, as Willow nudged her grey head into Dave's tanned, weather-roughened hands to get his attention.

"And here's Maya, she's our special girl, not used to people yet, but she's getting there, each day she's getting there," Patsy added, stepping to the side so Dave could see Maya hiding behind her legs.

At the sound of her name, Maya's ears twitched and she lifted her head a fraction, careful not to catch anyone's eye.

"Tom told me all about her when he rang, suggesting you all come down for the day... I'll leave her be, won't worry her with my fussing," Dave said, giving Willow's ears a final ruffle as he stood upright.

"Thanks for letting us come, I'm hoping it'll help

her, having a beach day's always fun isn't it?" Patsy said.

"It's a pleasure, really, least I can do. The beach hut's yours for the day, yours any day you want to come down in fact," Dave said, moving onto the decking and opening the white door of the blue painted wooden hut stood closest to them. Tom stepped forward and dropped the basket containing the day's food and drinks, just inside the door onto the pale, scrubbed wooden floorboards. With a sigh he slumped onto the narrow wooden bench which ran along the length of one wall and was covered with blue and white striped cushions; a matching striped table cloth, faded with age, lay on the neat wooden table in the middle of the compact space.

"Make yourself at home Tom!" Patsy smiled, as she stood in the doorway with Dave and the dogs.

"You bet I will. Love it here. This place hasn't changed at all. You've even got the same chipped china mugs," Tom said, nodding at the back wall where four blue and white mugs hung on hooks above the small sink.

"It's so quaint," Patsy smiled. "I've always wanted to see inside one of these little huts and when Tom told me he'd got a friend with one, well, let's just say you've made my day!"

"It's a great little place," Dave said. "Been in the family years, I've been coming here since I was a baby and Tom's had plenty of good trips down since we were kids at school together eh, Tom?"

"Certainly have, and a few chilly sea swims."

Dave grinned, "Don't advise dipping your toes in there today, it'll be nippy. This early in the season, the beach is nice and quiet, there won't be many folk about, you should have a good day. Right, will leave you all to it, got to get off."

"Sure you won't stay mate?" Tom asked.

"Would love to, but can't today, enjoy it, we'll catch up later."

Shortly after Dave had gone, Tom and Patsy were comfily sat on stripy cushions laid out on the decking, sipping tea, staring out across the wet sand at the turquoise sea, lapping gently at the shoreline. The tide was out, leaving a wide open, empty beach littered with pink and pearly-white shells and sea-polished grey-brown pebbles glistening in the sun. Willow was snuffling along the edge of the decking, her busy black nose turning yellow with sand as she breathed in and out rapidly, seeking out the source of the smell she'd detected. Maya's eyes followed her sister as her soft grey ears were ruffled by the gentle sea breeze. Every now and then, her nose twitched as it caught something on the salt-laden air, but she wasn't tempted to join in with the inquisitive sniffing that occupied her sister.

"Right, shall we see what Maya makes of the beach?" Patsy asked, taking Tom's empty mug from him as she moved to get up. Maya stood, taking a couple of steps backwards and Willow, seeing everyone was moving stopped investigating the smells under the decking and looked up, eager to join in with whatever was about to happen.

"Ok, let's go girls," Patsy grabbed both dog leads, stepped off the decking onto the sand, and with Tom they all set off across the beach towards the water.

94

Willow bounced along, excited by the shifting sand under her paws. Maya, wary of the new sensation moved cautiously, stopping after a few seconds to size things up. She looked up at Patsy, then over at Willow before turning her head back towards the safety of the hut. Overhead a seagull caught her eye and she tracked it as it flew across out over the sea, disappearing into the distance. Giving her a few minutes, Patsy and Tom stood quietly, allowing her to savour everything: each sight, sound and smell of the beach was new to Maya. Patsy saw her tail lift, her nose twitch and a new sense came over Maya: curiosity was drowning out anxiety.

Tom bent to unclip Willow's lead, freeing her to race ahead, and she sprang across the damp sand straight towards a clump of brown rubbery seaweed, into which she buried her nose, snorting in the briny scents. She came up for air and turned back to see where her sister was, threads of seaweed dripping from her face. Maya was stood still, watching, smelling, listening.

"Well, Willow's happy!" Patsy smiled. "What do you think, shall we?"

"Go on, she's ready I reckon. And there's nothing to worry about, we're safe here," Tom said, scanning the empty beach. "Besides she's going to stick with her sister there who's enjoying herself," Tom's eyes rested on Willow a few metres away, bottom in the air, nose pushing into the sand, moving her head from side to side to cover as much of her face with sand as she could.

Patsy knelt down beside Maya who was intently watching Willow giving herself the wet sandy face wash.

"Ok, this is it darling, first time off-lead, first real day of freedom to run… but not too far!"

As she unclipped Maya's lead, Patsy and Tom took a step to the side and watched as she shook herself from head to tail, sneezed loudly and walked across the sand to her sister. When Willow spotted Maya approaching, she promptly stopped messing about in the sand and bounced over to her, tail wagging happily. As she reached Maya, she play bowed, her bottom in the air, her head down looking up at Maya. Then, up and down Willow bounced in front of her sister, who took one look at her and slowly at first, her tail just beginning to twitch, mimicked her sister's bounces, getting faster as round and round in a loose circle they bobbed. Bottoms up, then down, paws patting the sand in front of each other, teasing, playing like normal, happy dogs.

"Oh my goodness, it's wonderful!" gasped Patsy, grabbing Tom's hand, tears of joy pricking her eyes. "Maya looks so happy, so normal, this is the first time she's ever been playful."

"She's being a dog. Simple as that! At last she knows what it is to be happy and is showing it. It's fab… and you're fab to have given her this chance at life," Tom smiled, wrapping his arm around Patsy's shoulder as they walked along following the playful dogs, running off towards the sparkling water a short distance away.

As the sisters shot across the wet sand, first one would stop, distracted by something and take a swift sniff, before the other quickly joined her, and two noses were then pushing in to get the best smell. Then, as fast as they stopped, off they rushed, running ahead, zig zagging across the wide beach before hurtling back to check on Patsy and Tom, whose beaming faces the dogs scanned before turning tail and zipping away again.

As they reached the shoreline together, both dogs skidded, their paws cleaving eight deep grooves into the sand as they came to a sudden halt. Hopping backwards to keep their paws clear of the lapping waves, they stood, side by side, matching noses high in the air, taking in the moist salty air.

"Do you reckon they'll go in?" Tom said as he and Patsy reached the water's edge.

"Not a chance! Willow hates being wet and I doubt Maya's any different, nor will she go in without her big sis."

No sooner were Patsy's words out of her mouth, than Willow and Maya both turned round and headed off back up the beach, distancing themselves from the chilly water.

"What did I say?" Patsy laughed.

Later, back at the hut, Willow and Maya lay on the seagrass matting, Willow's head resting on the soft cushion of Maya's body as they napped, exhausted by a morning of beach games and fun. Soft snores from both dogs matched Tom's, as he stretched outside in the deckchair in the afternoon sun. Patsy, propped against the hut's painted blue wall, which faced out to sea, watched over them all, smiling to herself as she looked at both dogs, their coats thick with sand, their faces mussed up and gritty. Patsy sighed, happy in the knowledge that the mess the dogs would take home with them was worth it. It made her eyes prick with happy tears as she thought of Maya so joyful and free, doing exactly as she pleased and, with the soft warmth of the sun on her face, Patsy closed her eyes and pledged that this was what Maya's life would always be from now on.

19

You know that place between sleep and awake, that place where you still remember dreaming? That's where I'll always love you. That's where I'll be waiting.

J.M. Barrie, *Peter Pan*

I woke before dawn today. I often do. Years of living in a disturbing din have left their mark on my sleeping habits. As I woke, I felt the warm, soft snoring body of Willow next to me. Willow, my beautiful, kind sister. Her warmth seeped into me, giving me a comforting peace I didn't want to disturb. So I lay still, matching the rhythm of my breathing with each of Willow's gentle snores:

ZZZZZ… in… zzzz… out… ZZZZZ… in… zzzz… out… ZZZZZ… peace… zzzz… in… ZZZZ… out… zzzz… ZZZ… peace…

Peaceful breaths… in… out. Such peace like I could never in my wildest dreams ever have thought I'd feel. Never, ever.

"YAARFFF!"

Just as I drifted back into sleep, Willow startled me and herself awake with a yawn, her wide open mouth revealing a set of perfect, gleaming white teeth, right next to my face.

"Morning precious," I said to my sister, I love having someone to say this to each day.

I'm impressed every time I see her perfect teeth, although there's a dash of sadness as I think about my own gummy mouth. One of the good things to happen to me – and there have been many since I was carried out of the puppy farm a few months ago – was the removal of my rotten, broken and aching teeth. Although it left me with many gaps and I've no front teeth on the bottom row, the pain I'd lived with for a very long time disappeared as if by magic. Dogs have forty-two teeth, so despite missing a few it still leaves enough for me to eat with.

Eating. Who would have thought eating can be so enjoyable? I've had a great number of tasty meals, since coming to live with Patsy and Willow. Every single thing that I've eaten here, has been tummy-tingling delicious. Patsy loves to cook, and I love to eat. We're a match well suited.

This is a funny thing, Willow's nibbling me, she wants me to join in with her daily game of *'wakey-wakey-chewy face'*. It's another lovely new moment I enjoy each day: when we wake, we stay in our bed and before Patsy stirs, nibble each other's faces. With small, soft nips of my ears, Willow begins the game just as she is now, and something stirs inside me, a deep, long forgotten memory of something like this when I was an itty-bitty puppy.

But the memory of that game is nothing like this; for one thing, we play while we're lying in this enormous, squishy bed that I've learnt is ours to share. When I first came, I slept on the floor, not knowing I could climb in with Willow each night. Now, I'm usually in there first, and I'm always last to leave each morning. I love the cushioned comfort around my body and sometimes I head back upstairs during the day, on my own, just to get back into the deep nest of a bed for a minute or two. Ooooh, the pleasure of sinking down into it is worth the stair climb, which can be a bit of a chore with my stiff hips. I've almost forgotten what it felt like to lay night after night on the hard concrete amid the dirt and dust of the horrible barn. Almost, but not quite.

Once Willow starts the nipping of my ears, I give

into the pleasure I get from her doing this, and soon start returning the nibbles. As my teeth are few, it's more like a gummy suck than a toothy chew, although we call it a game of *'chewy face'*. Over each other's faces we go: nip, nibble, tug and pull, mouthing with low mumbling sounds rising into our throats, from deep wells of doggy joy. As our enjoyment grows, so do the sounds and strength of nips. Most times, Willow ends up rolling onto her back with her legs in the air, paws twitching and tapping the air, and as the game reaches its climax, one of us usually gets a little too excited and the other feels the faint sting of a nip that's a little too nippy for comfort. And we stop. Happily played out. Set up for the rest of the day.

20

All shall be done, but it may be harder than you think.

C.S.Lewis,
The Lion, the Witch and the Wardrobe

"I need to see the vet please. Yes, soon as possible, it's an emergency," Patsy spoke into the phone with an urgency Willow hadn't heard before. Patsy was worried, so she was worried too. Maya was too ill to be worried.

Maya had been with them for several weeks and although things frightened her that Willow never gave a thought to – walking on the tiled kitchen floor had been terrifying for a couple of weeks – she'd seemed to be making good progress and feeling more confident by the day. Her health had been improving, she'd been getting stronger and her weight was good, she was no longer the skinny, fragile dog who'd been carried out of the puppy farm in the arms of kind rescuers.

It had all been going so well. And now it wasn't. Patsy was on the point of panic as overnight things had changed. Out of the blue, Maya started vomiting. Not just a small bit of sick, Willow did that sometimes and, disgusting as Patsy found it, she'd swiftly eat it up again, it was no big deal to Willow. But last night, Maya's sickness was different. She was properly ill and wouldn't touch her supper. Although at that point neither Patsy nor Willow were overly concerned, Patsy had hoped a good night's sleep and no evening meal would see things right by the morning. And as Patsy wasn't too anxious, Willow relaxed and secretly thought a small perk of having a sickly sister, was that she got to gobble up Maya's leftovers before Patsy could whip the uneaten meal away.

But, this morning Maya had not only turned down her breakfast, and been sick when she gulped some water, she'd emptied her bowels with a soggy pile of sloppy poo, which Willow, who normally enjoyed a quick inspection of other dogs' poop, hopped away from in horror. The smell was bad, rotten and not in a good way as some rotten stinks could be; in fact some, like fox poo, or even better, horse manure Willow found irresistible. No, there was nothing good today about the product of Maya's bottom, nothing good at all. There was something sinister about it. Since the first messy lake of slimy sludge, Maya's poops had been coming with more force and frequency. She hadn't even managed to get to the back door, let alone out into the garden, and as Patsy rushed to clear up the last messy pool on the tiles, she'd gasped in alarm as she saw it spreading across the floor, crimson with Maya's blood.

"Ok, we're on our way," Patsy slammed the phone onto the table, and grabbed Willow and Maya's leads. "Come on Willow, you'd best come with us, Maya will feel better if you're with her."

Maya, weak with exhaustion lay on the mat by the kitchen door, she was too poorly to move into her warm bed just a meter away in the corner.

"Oh sweetheart, don't worry, we'll get you better, promise we will," Patsy leaned down and scooped Maya's frail body into her arms. "I really know you're not yourself, there's no way you'd usually let me pick you up without a little squirm is there?" she nudged gently into Maya's neck with a soft kiss of comfort as she carried her to the car.

In the waiting room at the vet, Willow sat quietly fretting at Patsy's feet, while Maya lay shivering in her arms. What if Maya didn't get better? Yes, Patsy had promised she would, and so far, Patsy had never broken a promise, but, Willow knew Maya was dangerously ill. More ill than Willow had ever seen a dog. Even ancient, wrinkly Doris when she'd last been seen in Kettlecroft Park, the day before she died last winter, didn't poop like Maya had this morning, or look as ill as she did cradled in Patsy's arms. No, Willow desperately wanted to trust Patsy knew best, but, she had a bad feeling about this. Poor Maya had suffered so much in her life, her body had been battered and weakened so deeply over the years, that Willow wasn't sure her sister had the strength to pull through this time.

Willow's sadness and worry grew as she turned her head again to look up at her sister. She wanted nothing more than to take away Maya's pain, to nurse her back to health. She was overcome with a need to comfort her and stood up on her back legs, placing her paws on Patsy's knee, searching out her sister's face which was nestled deep in the green, knitted blanket she was wrapped up in. As their noses touched, Willow gave her sister's muzzle a soft, slow lick of comfort.

"Be strong Maya. Please be strong. You'll be all right. You'll see, the vet'll get you better. He will, really, promise he will," she whispered, hoping from the bottom of her heart that what she said was true.

"Come through," she heard a male voice above her as Patsy stood up and, with Maya in her arms they all followed the young vet in blue scrubs along the corridor into his consulting room. Willow tried hard not to be alarmed by the bombardment of clinical smells and bright lights. She knew this was where her sister needed to be. It smelt of efficiency.

The vet listened intently as Patsy rattled through events, giving detailed descriptions of Maya's symptoms, and her past.

"She's a dog who's really not had a good life, she's suffered more than we can imagine," she said, stroking Maya's neck as the dog lay on the steel examination table.

The vet asked a few more questions, took Maya's temperature and examined her with gentle, confident hands.

"Mmm, she's in a lot of pain poor girl, but we can help that," he said, preparing the first of a few injections. "I'm giving her something for the pain which will start working now, and I'll send you home with pills to give her over the next few days. I'm also giving something to settle her sickness and diarrhoea."

"Is she going to be ok?" Patsy anxiously asked,

carefully wrapping Maya in her arms to lift her down from the table. She stood her on the floor with Willow, who immediately shuffled closer, to be as near as she could to her sister, seeking to comfort her with the closeness of her body.

"She will, yes, so long as you give her the pills, and watch her closely over the next 24 hours," the vet handed Patsy a small packet, "she has a nasty tummy bug, but with what I've just given her, and your swift action today bringing her in, she should be well on the road to recovery by tomorrow. But, if she gets any worse, or continues vomiting, or you're worried at all, you must bring her straight back. But, really I think she's best off with you at home for now."

Patsy gave a huge sigh of relief, "Oh my goodness, thank you, I'm SO thankful… I've been frantic thinking we might lose her."

"Really, she's not out of the woods, but I'm sure she's going to be fine, she's a fighter this little one," the vet said, opening the consulting room door for Patsy and dogs.

Outside by the car, Patsy knelt down close to Maya, and whispered, "Come on, let's get you both home, you're going to be ok, I promise." Willow nuzzled into the other side of Patsy's face and gave a low, throaty noise of agreement. Wrapping her arm around Willow, bringing her in closer still, Patsy felt a single tear of love-filled relief slide down her cheek. "If only you both knew how much you mean to me, and how much I love you both," she whispered.

"Gosh, it's such a relief," she said to Tom on the phone

later that evening, "she's doing miles better tonight than she was earlier. There's been no sickness now since this morning. Whatever magic medicine the vet gave her seems to have done the trick. Thank goodness, I was so worried, when I saw the blood, I honestly thought we were going to lose her."

"Good news!" Tom said, "She's had more than her share of suffering in her life, must have been horrible seeing her so poorly."

"It really was, but, the vet said she's a fighter, and she certainly is. Guess that helped keep her alive all those years in the puppy farm. So sad. But, we're not thinking about that now, she doesn't need me to dwell on any of that... she's getting better, that's all that matters."

"And how's Willow coped?"

Patsy looked down at Willow, who was nestled in bed with Maya, her sleeping head resting on Maya's bottom, "She's been a star, she really has. She's not left Maya's side all day."

"Perfect!" Tom said. "You couldn't have hoped for closer sisters could you?"

"Not at all, they're special, really special together," Patsy smiled, her heart warm at the closeness of her dogs, and her love for them both.

21

You cannot stop the birds of sorrow from flying over your head, but you can stop them nesting in your hair.

Eva Ibbotson, *The Dragonfly Pool*

In the puppy farm I had to learn ways to survive. If I hadn't, I would not have lasted all those years. I think this helped to pull me through my recent sickness, that plus the love and care given to me by Patsy and Willow.

Some of the dogs in the puppy farm never did learn to cope and their lives were short and terrible. We were all there to produce puppies for the Man. That's all. It sounds simple, but it's not. It's horrible and nasty. When we didn't produce puppies we disappeared. The Man no longer had use of us. He kept only those that gave him what he wanted: puppies to sell.

I knew all through those long years that it wasn't the life I should have been living. I don't know how I knew it, perhaps it was my ancestors calling down through the ages to me, urging me to struggle on, to survive so that one day my true life would begin. And now it has, and

I'm loving it and will fight to stay and enjoy it for as long as I can.

I've been living with my precious and wonderful sister Willow for quite a few months. It's been hard at times to adjust and learn how to live this life, the one my instincts told me one day would be mine if only I could hang on, and survive the horror of the puppy farm a bit longer, and a bit longer till the fateful day of my rescue arrived.

Willow's helped me to know what humans are really like. They're truly kind. Not at all like the Man. I was wary of Tom at first, his deep male voice rattled in my head, stirring memories of the barn and the Man. I think I made him work hard at gaining my trust; not that I meant to, I just couldn't help myself cowering away if he came near to me. But, he is kind and patient and in those early, difficult days seemed to understand that I was doing my best. My struggles to cope with all the new sounds and smells, people and places, didn't faze Tom at all, he is a good man.

Patsy has been marvellous. She really has understood most of my needs and allowed me to take all the time I've needed to learn everything I have. Willow's curiosity about my past is strong and I've given her a few snippets of detail when she's pressed me to tell her. But really I haven't wanted to upset her with my bad memories which will haunt her innocent mind. She's often pressed me to tell her something about my puppies, so, after much reluctance, for fear of upsetting her sweet innocence, one day I gave in and told her of the first time they were taken from me.

It was a cold day, freezing in the barn, and it haunts me all these years on. I'd just finished feeding them, all six tiny pups of mine were scrambling about, playing together as best they could in the empty concrete pen which was our home. I was young then, I'd not long grown out of my own puppyhood and I had more energy and milk than with my later litters. I fed my babies well and they were growing bigger every day.

Then, suddenly the Man entered the pen, dropping a plastic box down hard on the ground, startling me and my puppies. Before we knew what was happening, he grabbed the closest one by her back leg taking her by surprise. She was always first to push in for a feed from me and was the plumpest one of my babies. I helplessly watched her soft tiny body, wriggling in his hands, saw him squeeze her tightly to keep her still while snarling nasty words at her, as she frantically tried to get free from his big, cruel fists. He roughly dropped her into the box, slamming down the lid to stop her escaping. My mind reeled as I struggled to understand what was happening, then he made a grab for her little brother, who had jumped behind me to hide. A sharp pain shot through my ribs, as the Man pushed me aside with his dirty black boot, grabbing my boy's tail, lifting him up swiftly and putting him in the box with his sister. As I gasped for breath through the searing pain, all the while I could hear her inside the box, squealing with fright, and I knew I couldn't help her. After a few minutes, he'd caught all my puppies, opened the steel gate and slammed it shut again, as he disappeared with the box full of my crying babies. I was left alone in the pen, shaking with shock and pain, their squealing cries ringing in my ears.

I worried for days and days about them, hoping he'd bring them back to me. I missed them terribly. I ached with misery at their hasty, brutal disappearance. Then, after about a week I had no choice but to accept they weren't coming back and that they were gone forever.

As I told Willow this tale, her face full of sorrow, I wished I hadn't given her the harsh truth of my life. I instantly regretted sharing my sadness. But, as is always the case with my jolly, confident sister, after a few moments of sad thoughts, and a comforting snuggle with me, she was up and bouncing around looking for a toy to start a game with. That's the wonder of Willow, nothing keeps her down for long. She's always lively, determined each day to enjoy herself. She knows this is what her life is all about, and is great at sharing her enthusiasm with me. I've learned so many things about being a normal, happy dog since living with her.

There's so much simple joy in Willow's world which is now my world too, it's truly ours to share: daily walks with Patsy and Tom, friends and games in Kettlecroft Park, ample good food, trips to the beach, toys to chew and chuck about, and when all that's done, we retreat into the peace and quiet comfort of our bed. I'm absorbing every one of these treasured moments at Willow's side, and I bask in her glow of happiness, allowing myself to forget the darkness of my past. With her help, I'm learning that trusting Patsy is a good idea, as she'll always look out for us and keep us both safe and happy. Seeing how Willow cuddles up with her, so naturally and with such pleasure,

I'm slowly being tempted to follow my sister's example and do the same. Only, I can't quite let myself, not yet. But I know I will. And one day, one day very soon, I'll know I'm a deep-down, thoroughly healed, rescued dog, ready to make the most of my happy life full of exciting adventures with my sister Willow.

Dear reader,

This book is based on the lives of real dogs who were rescued from awful situations but who eventually got to live happily in their new homes. If you'd like to have a dog in your life - and this ought to be something the whole family agrees on - please first look into adopting one from a good rescue. It may take a little bit of time and patience, but that's good, how it should be as bringing dogs into our lives is something we should think long and hard about. If you do buy a puppy, don't rush into it and do research it well; when you find a good breeder, check mum and puppies are all well cared for, happy and healthy and mum is with her puppies when you visit. Never buy a puppy from a petshop, or have one delivered to you.

Thank you for reading and caring,

Janetta

Acknowledgements

This book has been made possible by the support of many people, our friends and families, including Renae, Twinkle, Cerise, Susie-Belle, Alfie and Reeva. And a tremendous thank you to all the generous individuals who backed our Kickstarter campaign and trusted us. We sincerely thank each of you and hope you know that you will have helped to save dogs in no small way, as this book reaches young readers for years to come.

Special thanks to:

Bee O'Wulf; Sylvia Buxcey; Heather Godwin; Claire Farrington; Graeme Goode; Joelle Hoggan; Mike Jackson; Melinda Carroll; Caroline Mace; Elizabeth Bolt; Joanna Taylor; Pamela and Keith Knight; Dawn Wharrad; Kim E. Barrett; Charlotte Mackaness; Jan Tomalin; Siobhan Wing; Karen Doonan; Celeste Barrett; Maureen Jacques; Carol Sykes; Amanda Jones; Amanda Pearce; Gemma Ridley; Rhian White; Camilla Kinton; Rachel Williams; Janet North; Schnauzer Forum UK; Colleen, Will, Owen and Haatchi.

Finally, for lending us their superb skills and being patient when we were giving in to giggles, Tamara Panchen and Charley Surrage.

If you like the idea of sharing your life with a dog, it's a big decision to make. To help you be sure that it's the right thing for you and most importantly for the dog, here are some questions to ask yourself:

Why do you want to share your life with a dog?

When we bring a dog into our life we're making a commitment to look after them for their whole lifetime, which could be many years. They're completely reliant on us to take care of them for all that time. It's never like having a new toy, or game, something that can be forgotten about when the novelty fades. A dog is a special friend who we must promise to care for and love for years and years. Even when they're old, in fact it's never more important than when they become our elderly friends to love them and do everything for them that they need us to. And if we do so, in all the years we have together, we'll share much happiness and fun. But we must be serious about the commitment involved.

Are you ready to do all the jobs a dog will need you to do?

It's a good idea to make a list of what you think a dog will need you to do. I'll start you off: feeding is important, and so are daily walks, even if it's raining, or you don't really feel like going out. What will happen for holidays? Will you share the tasks with someone else? If so, what happens if they don't feel like doing it one day? A dog never likes to be left alone for hours on end, how will you be sure this won't happen? Remember Charlie and how his life wasn't always happy because his first families didn't give him the time and attention he needed? Can you be certain you'll always be there for your dog and never, ever let him down?

Do you know that someone will pay for everything your dog might need?

Remember when Maya was sick and had to visit the vet? This kind of thing can happen to any dog and can be costly. Or the puppy Beebee, who was bought and fell ill soon afterwards? We need to be certain we can afford to pay unexpected bills for our dogs throughout their lifetime, remember they rely on us completely.

Are you sure you can have a dog where you live?

Not all places allow dogs. What happens if you move? Are you certain your dog will always go with you, and that you'll never move somewhere that a dog isn't allowed?

Even if we can't share our lives with dogs, there are many ways to enjoy being with them and helping those in need. Visiting your local rescue shelter will give you ideas for what you can do to help. They always rely on fundraising and volunteers to make the lives of animals in their care the best they can be.

To find out more about buying and adopting dogs, helping those like Maya, and what we can all do to make the lives of dogs better, I'd love you to visit my website where you'll also find a special page for young readers:

www.janettaharvey.com

Sit
Think
Dream
and let
The Magic
Appear...